OSSIE GOES SUPERSONIC!

CW00840290

Also available in Young Lions

Sunshine Island, Moonshine Baby *Clare Cherrington*
Flossie Teacake's Fur Coat *Hunter Davies*
Flossie Teacake – Again! *Hunter Davies*
Flossie Teacake Strikes Back! *Hunter Davies*
Come On, Ossie *Hunter Davies*
Ghosts and Shadows *Dorothy Edwards (ed.)*
The Lily Pickle Band Book *Gwen Grant*
The Return of the *Antelope Willis Hall*
The *Antelope* Company Ashore *Willis Hall*
The *Antelope* Company at Large *Willis Hall*
Challenge in the Dark *Robert Leeson*
The Demon Bike Rider *Robert Leeson*
Wheel of Danger *Robert Leeson*

Ossie Goes Supersonic!

HUNTER DAVIES

Illustrated by
MALOU

Young Lions

First published in Great Britain 1986
by The Bodley Head Ltd
First published in Young Lions 1988
8 Grafton Street, London W1X 3LA

Young Lions is an imprint of
the Children's Division, part of
the Collins Publishing Group

Text copyright © 1986 by Hunter Davies
Illustrations copyright © 1986 by Malou

Printed and bound in Great Britain by
William Collins Sons & Co. Ltd, Glasgow

Conditions of Sale
This book is sold subject to the condition
that it shall not, by way of trade or otherwise,
be lent, re-sold, hired out or otherwise circulated
without the publisher's prior consent in any form of
binding or cover other than that in which it is
published and without a similar condition
including this condition being imposed
on the subsequent purchaser.

CONTENTS

1

Ossie and the Phone-In

Ossie was on the phone. He was actually sitting on the phone, at least the receiver part. He had dialled the number some time ago and had been told to hang on, so he had put the phone between his legs, just in case it fell off the stool where he was sitting.

He needed both hands free because he wasn't just phoning—he was having his breakfast, putting on his shoes, thinking deep thoughts about the world, reading that morning's copy of *Shoot*, ignoring his sister Lucy who was being a pain as usual, listening to the radio, watching breakfast television, and every sixty seconds, when he remembered, he was doing his muscle-forming exercises. His grandad had told him that if you breathed in, held your breath for a count of ten, and tightened each arm muscle, then you would notice a miraculous improvement.

"Load of rubbish," muttered Ossie, going almost blue in the face as he held his breath and examined his upper arm for any signs of life, never mind growth. "It's never gonna work. I should have been Superman by now, with all this effort."

"What you holding up those match sticks for, Ossie?" It was Lucy. He had hoped she hadn't seen him. He preferred to do his muscle-forming exercises in the privacy of his bedroom, but last night he had forgotten. In fact he'd forgotten for a whole week. He had a lot of muscle-forming to catch up on.

"Ha ha ha," said Ossie. "Just you shurrup."

Lucy was packing her bag for school, all very neat as usual. She already had her coat on and her money for the day and the note she had to return and her stuff for PE. Ossie was still half undressed.

"You should get up earlier in the morning," said Lucy.

"You should get lost," said Ossie.

Ossie hated people telling him what to do, especially his younger sister, but slowly his mind drifted back over the pages of *Shoot*, with only half an eye now on the television and just part of an ear on the radio, while at the same time he finished his Coco Pops. He paused to feel his right bicep, just in case miracles might be happening.

"Please hold on for another few seconds . . ."

Immediately Ossie dropped his comic and flexed his arm muscles, both at once, which was agony for him, then he realized it had been a voice on the telephone.

He'd forgotten about the phone.

"Stupid operator," said Ossie. "I don't know why I bother. They've been asking all morning for people to ring in, then when I do, they just tell me to wait. They must think I'm a right idiot."

"You are," said Lucy.

Ossie threw the Coco Pops packet across the kitchen table, just missing her as she went out of the door.

"Bye Mum," shouted Lucy. "Have a nice day, Mum!"

"Creep," said Ossie. "Double creep."

"Oswald Osgood, what are you doing?"

It was Ossie's mum. Like Lucy, she had her coat on, all ready to go off to work.

"Lots of things," said Ossie. "You know how clever I am."

"And what are you doing with that phone?"

"Er, holding it. Just keeping it warm. Gets rather cold this time of the morning."

"Don't try to be clever with me," said his mother, grabbing the receiver from Ossie, and holding it to her ear.

"*Right then, pop picker of the day, let's have your fave rave, because this very moment, you lucky person, you're talking to Radio Century, the grooviest local radio station in the entire universe . . .*"

"Wrong number," said Ossie quickly, seizing the phone and banging down the receiver.

"What have you been up to?" said his mother angrily. "You've been ringing that ridiculous radio programme, haven't you? Don't you realize it costs a fortune! This is the peak time. What's more, you're going to be late for school . . ."

Ossie's mother had him by the arm and forced him off the stool, then stood over him as he laced up his shoes.

"Comic," said his mother.

"That's right," said Ossie, very cheekily.

"You've got it in one . . . Ouch, stop it."

"Bowl," said his mother, still standing over him. Ossie resisted the temptation to be clever this time.

It was the rule in the Osgood household that each person made his own breakfast and cleared up his own dishes afterwards. After all, his mother went to work, so she could not be expected to run after Ossie and Lucy. They were now aged twelve and ten, old enough to look after themselves, though his mother did have her doubts about Ossie.

Ossie slowly put away his comics, cleared the table and put his dirty dishes in the dishwasher, unplugged the TV and switched off the radio.

"I'm just a skivvy in this house," said Ossie. "Won't be able to do any school work after this. Me brain's worn out. As for me muscles . . ."

"Oh, stop going on about your muscles."

"Do you think I'll have any when I'm eighteen, Mum. Honestly?"

"Look, just concentrate on one thing at a time. That's your problem, Ossie. You will let your mind wander. Do one thing, and do it properly, that's my advice to you."

Ossie got his school things on, and his bag ready

while his mother watched.

"Right, have you got everything at last?"

"Just one thing, Mum," said Ossie, pretending to think hard. Then he grabbed hold of his mother.

"One cuddle, that's all."

Ossie gave his mother a bear hug, almost poking her eye out as his sports bag swung round her head.

He liked giving his mother cuddles, but he preferred doing it when Lucy wasn't there to watch.

Miss Turkey, Ossie's form teacher, was going round the class, giving back the English essays.

"About time," whispered Ossie to Desmond, his best friend.

"Yeh," said Desmond, "she's had them yonkers."

"She's so lazy, that woman," said Ossie. "I could have marked them in half the time."

"Probably never read them," said Desmond.

"Mine was pretty good," said Ossie. "Lot of long words. Probably hard for her to understand, she is so thick."

Ossie felt his ear being grabbed.

"What did you say, Oswald Osgood?"

Miss Turkey had come round behind the tables, while Ossie and Desmond were chattering to each other. She usually called him Ossie, as most people did, and the sound of his full Christian name, which Ossie hated, meant trouble.

"Me, Miss? Not me, Miss. Never said nuffink, Miss."

"Two negatives do not make an affirmative, Ossie."

"Yes, Miss, I mean no, Miss."

"I distinctly heard you. 'She is so thick.' To whom did that refer, pray?"

Ossie thought for a long time, then he smiled.

"She's so quick," said Ossie. "That's what I said. I meant Flossie Teacake. She's always so quick at doing her work, reading and writing, and stuff like that . . ."

Flossie Teacake, a rather plump girl who was sitting on the other side of Ossie, dug him in the ribs with her elbow.

"Don't bring me into this," she said.

"That's enough of that," said Miss Turkey.

She was about to give Ossie his essay, but then she decided to keep it in her hand. Flossie got hers back, and so did Desmond.

"Heh, brill," shouted Desmond. "Really mass. Look at this, Ossie, I got B plus, my best mark ever. I bet that's the best in the class."

Flossie smirked, tossing her hair, peering over her specs, trying to look superior. Sometimes, thought Ossie, I hate that girl. She must have got a better mark, but she wasn't letting on, not until someone asked her, which Ossie certainly was not going to do.

"Whatcha get, Ossie?" said Desmond.

"She's holding on to it," growled Ossie. "Probably gonna read it out to the whole class. It was pretty good."

"Pretty useless, I bet."

"No, it was really good, my longest ever. She said do only three pages but I did, I dunno, must have been three and a quarter pages. My hands weren't half aching. I wouldn't be surprised if it was going on show, in the manuscript room of the British Museum with Wandsworth and Shirley . . ."

"Wordsworth and Shelley," said Flossie. "You always get everything wrong, Ossie Osgood."

"Belt up, Four Eyes," said Ossie.

This time Flossie gave him a push. As she was rather heavier, rather taller, rather stronger, than Ossie, he almost fell off his chair.

"Come out here, Ossie Osgood," said Miss Turkey.

Ossie noticed that Miss Turkey was holding up his essay, so he got up from behind the table, beginning to smile.

"See, she's gonna to read it out," he said to Desmond. "You was wrong, clever clogs. Let me out. Bet it's an A."

"I have refused to mark this essay," announced Miss Turkey in her poshest, bossiest voice.

"'Cos it's too clever for you to understand," muttered Ossie.

He was pushing his way to the front, which was pretty difficult because his enemies, as well as most of his friends, were sticking out their feet or their bags or their chair legs, trying to block his passage or trip him up, but going all innocent every time he struggled to get past.

"I will not, repeat not, have work like this handed in. The contents may be first class, for all I know, but it is impossible for me to judge."

"It is actually," said Ossie. "Alpha plus plus, if you ask me."

"No one is asking you—except one thing. In future, boy, I want your essays written out properly. I have never seen such filthy, untidy work. And look at these stains. Did you eat your breakfast off it? And as for the handwriting, it is abysmal."

Miss Turkey held the pages out with the tippy tips of her fingers as if she might become contaminated.

Ossie took the essay from her. She gave a little shudder, glad to get rid of the offending pages.

"My advice to you, boy, is to smarten yourself up."

Ossie went back to his place, muttering to himself.

He could sense Flossie and everyone else sniggering. Even Desmond, his best friend, was smiling.

"That's all I ever get given in this stupid world," thought Ossie to himself. "Stupid advice . . ."

It was Saturday morning and Ossie had just finished doing his grandad's weekend shopping. His grandfather lived in Sheltered Housing, a little flat in a new, purpose-built block. He lived alone, apart from all his worldly possessions, most of which he had crammed into his bedroom. If Ossie was very good, he was sometimes allowed to see his grandad's wartime treasures.

Ossie was feeling tired because the two plastic bags from Tesco were both very full. He had one in each hand and he felt as if his arms were getting longer all the time. He'd gone to a big supermarket for once, in the middle of the town, instead of the smaller one near Grandad's flat. It was all Grandad's fault. He'd heard that sugar in Tesco was 2p cheaper this week.

"If only I was eighteen," thought Ossie. "I could carry ten bags like this, without feeling a thing. I wonder if I'll ever grow. I've been like this for yonkers. It's not fair."

He put his bags down on the pavement and leaned against a wall.

"Fact I think I'm getting smaller, if you ask me, not that anyone asks me anything."

At that moment a large black limousine drew up, with a uniformed driver in front. A young lady, with long blonde hair, leaned out of the back window.

"I say, young man."

"Whatchawant," said Ossie, grunting. He didn't like strangers addressing him as young man, when it was obvious to the whole world that he was a small boy, and a pretty weedy one at that. He'd probably never make it to a man, young or otherwise, not the way nature was shaping him so far.

"We're looking for Radio Century."

"You what?" said Ossie, putting on his stupid face, but knowing perfectly well what the lady had said.

"We're going on their Saturday phone-in programme. You probably know it. Jolly popular round these parts, so I'm told."

"What parts?" said Ossie, looking round, keeping up his half-witted expression.

He noticed that a dog was just about to lift its leg and water Grandad's three bags of granulated sugar, special offer, 2 pee off. He managed to pick up both plastic bags, just in time.

"You mean Ziggy's agony programme," said Ossie. "I heard them trailing it this morning."

"Yes, that's right. How terribly clever of you to know."

19

"Are you Ziggy, then?" said Ossie.

"Of course not," said the girl, turning to someone sitting beside her. Ossie seemed to recognize the person from last night's Wogan programme. He had yellow hair, pulled back with a ribbon, and wore a multi-coloured satin shirt. He'd written some sort of book of Advice for Young People.

"Look, Caroline," snarled Ziggy. "Stop frigging around with this idiot. I wanna get back to London, pronto."

Ossie decided he didn't like Ziggy.

"We just want to find," said Caroline, enunciating her words slowly, "hold on, yes, Radio Century. If you listen to the programme, you must know where it is."

She picked up a clip board from her bag.

"Let me see now," she said, reading through her notes. "We've done Radio Oxford, that was the first thing, or was it Chiltern Radio? Never mind, we're here now, wherever we are. Ha ha ha. It's Radio Century at twelve. Super. Then Capital Radio at two o'clock. Nao problema. Though it could be pretty hairy, getting back to London in time if we can't find . . ."

"This is the last time I'm going on tour with a goddam Sloane," said Ziggy, slumping back in his seat.

"Radio Century?" said Ossie, going all bright-eyed and intelligent at last. "I know it very well. There's only one problem."

"What's that?" said Caroline.

"On strike," said Ossie. "All out at eleven o'clock this morning. Very sudden. I heard it on the news. That's it for the whole weekend. Complete shut-down. I'm pretty fed up myself, 'cos I always listen to their football reports at . . ."

"That's it then," said Ziggy, tapping the chauffeur on the shoulder. "London first stop, mate. This bleedin' town gives me the creeps."

The car raced away, tyres screeching. Ossie bent down and picked up his shopping, sighing to himself. He even managed to break into a trot, which was most surprising, considering how heavy his bags were. Had those muscle-forming exercises helped his biceps at last?

★

"Right then, Grandad," shouted Ossie from the hall. "So you've got everything. OK? No need to pay me now. Next week will do."

Ossie had put all Grandad's shopping away neatly, something he usually forgot to do. He had even opened a can of Guinness for him, placing it on the arm of his favourite chair, and brought him a packet of salt and vinegar crisps.

Grandad was now waiting for Jimmy Greaves and Ian St John to appear on the TV. He hated both of them, so he maintained, and shouted at them all the time they were on, but he never missed them every Saturday lunchtime.

"Are you listening, Grandad? I'm off now. Is that clear?"

Ossie opened the front door of Grandad's flat, then banged it as hard as he could.

Ossie listened carefully. He was still inside the flat. He could hear Grandad turning up the sound of the TV even more, complaining to himself about these people who would bang doors.

Very slowly, Ossie tiptoed back down the little hall and gently opened the door of Grandad's bedroom.

★

The whole of Grandad's bedroom was covered in wartime relics and mementoes but it was all so dark and gloomy that it took Ossie a long time to focus his eyes. There were bundles of old newspapers, tied up with string, boxes with letters sticking out of them, shelves piled high with dusty files and faded photographs.

Ossie was making for the wardrobe, picking his way carefully over and around all the jumble on the floor. He thought he could see a holster, with a pistol inside it, and a sheath with a dagger, but he avoided them, just in case he stood on anything dangerous.

The last time Ossie had looked inside the massive, old-fashioned wardrobe, something remarkable had happened. Or had he just imagined it? It had all been very peculiar.

He stepped inside the wardrobe and the door creaked slowly shut behind him.

He could still see a few chinks of light, through some cracks in the woodwork, and by using his hands he could feel some old uniforms, making out ribbons and badges, and the cold leather of what must be riding boots.

Ossie's hands suddenly grasped a very large, very heavy, leather belt, with a huge ornamental buckle. Very slowly, he hung it round his waist, though it could have gone round him twice. He was so small and the belt seemed so enormous.

"Oh, I wish I was eighteen," said Ossie. "It's not fair."

There was a strong smell of mothballs and old clothes, polish and perhaps even gunpowder. He was beginning to feel a bit dizzy. He closed his eyes, breathing in deeply.

"If I was eighteen now, I could wear some of this stuff. If I was eighteen now, I could, oh I could . . ."

When Ossie opened his eyes again, an amazing thing had happened. The belt now fitted perfectly.

He stepped out of the wardrobe and looked at himself in the mirror. Before him stood a tall, well built young man of eighteen, broad-shouldered, strong-armed, possibly even in need of a shave. He smiled, and the eighteen-year-old face smiled back. He felt the belt. It went exactly round his broad waist.

Inside, he was still Ossie, a first-year, twelve-year-old schoolboy, but outside, he was Oz.

He stood in the hall and listened again. The television was still blaring away. Grandad had heard nothing.

He very carefully opened the front door and went out, closing it quietly behind him, taking great care to lower his head.

When you're eighteen, and a good six foot high, you have to be careful of doorways in Sheltered Housing for the elderly.

Oz took the lift up to the fourth floor, as indicated on the notice board in the front hall of Century House. There were lots of other business offices in the block, but as it was Saturday, they were all closed. Only Radio Century, which had the entire fourth floor, was hard at work.

A girl with highly coloured make-up was on the switchboard behind a reception desk, talking on the phone to her boyfriend. A security guard was sitting beside her, drinking from a paper cup and ticking horses in the racing pages of the *Daily Mirror*.

Oz stood for a moment, looking at all the bright posters of Radio Century's famous disc jockeys and presenters. He knew most of their names, if not all their faces.

He was trying to decide whether to speak to the girl on the phone, or the security man, though neither seemed interested in him, when a very fraught-looking bald man, tall and thin, wearing a silk neckerchief, rushed out from what appeared to Oz to be a blank wall. There must have been a door he hadn't noticed.

"Ziggy! Thank God you're here. I was just going to ring your publishers. Where's Caroline?"

"Oh, she's not here," said Oz. His own deep voice rather took him by surprise.

"What a shame. She usually comes with all her authors."

"She had to go back to London," said Oz. "Some panic at the Bodley Feet headquarters. You know what it's like, man."

Oz wished he had listened more carefully to the way Ziggy spoke.

"Oh I say, that's good. Bodley Feet. Is that the latest in London? We're a bit out of touch up here."

He had only just managed to catch a glimpse of the clip board on Caroline's knee. It seemed to say "Bodley Feet Publishers" at the top in large blue letters, but it could have been Bodley Leg or Bodley Arm or even Bodily Harm.

"I'm going to be your producer," said the man. "It was going to be Mike, but he's out on a job, and Sarah's ill today and Pete's on leave, oh we're in a hell of a mess. So I'm afraid I haven't *quite* finished your book, but it looks trific, really good."

"Don't worry," said Oz. "I haven't read it either."

He thought for a moment that he'd said the wrong thing, but the producer laughed and slapped him on the back.

"That's ace, really ace."

The producer led Oz into a little studio, and pointed to where Oz should sit down.

"It's a self op, I'm afraid," said the producer.

"What?" said Oz, becoming slightly worried. "Not a hospital, is it? I don't want no operation. I had enough trouble with my tonsils and my mum said if ever . . ."

The producer was busy fitting some headphones to a plug under the table and wasn't really listening to Oz.

"We should really have an SM, but you know what it's like on a Saturday."

"Yeh well, most Scout Masters are out on Saturdays," said Oz.

"What?" said the producer, then he laughed, thinking he had missed another smart London joke.

"I was at BH for a time," he said, "in my salad days."

"You were in the canteen, were you?" said Oz, trying to remember if there still was a shop called Bourne and Hollingsworth, or had it closed. His mother had told him about it. Or did BH stand for Bodley Harm or Bodley Head, that stupid publishing firm. Must be stupid, to employ Caroline.

"Right, all systems go," said the producer. "Let's get the show on the road. Just a couple of commercials, then I'll announce you, give the number to ring, play another jingle, then the calls will start coming through. When the green comes on, it's all yours. But I don't need to tell you this, Ziggy. Ha ha ha. I know you've done this scores of times . . ."

"Scores," said Oz, beginning to feel slightly nervous. "Radio Oxford, Radio Chiltern, Radio Times, Radio Rentals, I've done them all. I think."

Oz was looking down at the headphones, knowing he had to put them on, but not quite sure which way they went. The producer meanwhile had gone out of the little room and reappeared behind a glass partition. He was busy at what looked like a giant keyboard of an electric organ, pulling switches, turning knobs. Oz could see him clearly, but was unable to hear anything. He seemed to be waving, so Oz waved back.

"Friendly people, in local radio," said Oz to himself.

The producer was still waving. Oz waved again, then he realized he was being waved at to pick up the headphones.

He put them on top of his head, but they fell over his nose and got mixed up with his necklace. Oz hadn't realized till then that he was wearing a necklace. Quite common of course, when you're eighteen. He felt his ears, one at a time, just in case he might be the sort of teenager who wore ear-rings. No.

The headphones then got mixed up with his belt, catching on the buckle, and he had to unwind all the wires. He could see the producer still waving at him.

"Good job I had my belt on. Could have lost this

little lot on the floor otherwise."

At length he got the headphones on. They felt uncomfortable pressing against his ears, but the moment he got them on he could hear everything loud and clear.

". . . and we're very honoured today to have live, in our studio, Ziggy, author of *Agony Uncle* which as you know is now zooming up the best-seller lists. He'll take any calls from any of you guys and dolls out there who want to ring in with your personal problems."

From his racy voice, thought Oz, you would never tell that the producer was bald and thin and scruffy and must be at least, well, almost forty years old.

"My name is Sid from Southfields," said a voice in Oz's ear. "And my problem is my garden. As I get older I find I can't do the digging as well. And cutting the grass really hurts my back. My children used to help me but now they say they won't unless they get paid. What should I do?"

"I get a lot of problems like this," said Oz. "On no account should you let any children under the age of eighteen do any gardening, certainly not boys. Let girls do it, they're much stronger. Boys of say twelve need to have lots of rests and big breakfasts and people not moaning at them and telling them what to do. Is that clear, Sid?"

"Oh, thank you very much, Ziggy . . ."

"If they *insist* on helping you, and some young boys are very kind, then on no account pay them less than five pounds an hour. With lots of drinks of Coke and chips and Big Macs, which *you* have to pay for. All right?"

"Oh, very good, I never thought of that."

"And the final solution, if that doesn't work, is concrete. Just concrete over your whole back garden. There's too many horrid vegetables being grown in this town as it is, all the cabbage and lettuce and yucky stuff. I even saw some radishes and beetroot when I was driving here today in my Rolls Royce."

"Oh, that is kind, Mr Ziggy. I never thought of that. Can I have a dedication?"

"What do you think this is—a funeral parlour?"

With that Oz cut the man off. He hadn't actually meant to, but he must have touched one of the little

32

buttons in front of him.

Through the headphones, he could hear the producer giving out the station's number, then playing another pop song, saying that Ziggy would be back on the line in just two minutes to answer more of your poy-son-al questions.

Oz was worried that he'd been a bit rude, but he was quite enjoying himself. It was like a game, as if he was talking to himself, all alone in his own room. He was used to doing that anyway. Lucy was always saying she could hear Ossie in his bedroom, having conversations with himself. All that experience was now proving very useful.

"My name is Sally from Palace Road and my problem is my two children . . ."

"That sounds like a pleasure to me," said Oz, "not a problem."

"Oh, yes, Ziggy, they can be a pleasure some-times, Ziggy, by the way is that your real name? I've always wondered. I've read all your books and I like that column you do in *Woman's Own*, or is it *Woman and Home*?"

"*Shoot*, actually," said Oz, "I write every story in

33

Shoot, and also the *Beano*, under other names of course."

"I'll have to get *Shoot* then, Ziggy. Does it come out Mondays or Thursdays . . .?"

"Look, do get on with it, Missus. There's hundreds of people waiting to talk to me. You're just twitting on like an old hen. My time is rather precious."

"Oh sorry, I quite forgot, it's so wonderful talking to you. Yes, they're very untidy my children. You wouldn't believe the state of their rooms. I keep telling them to clear up all the rubbish and throw out all the old comics, but they never do. What can I do about it?"

"Nothing is the answer. Your children didn't choose to have you for a mum. They didn't ask to be born."

"Oh, that's very true, Ziggy."

"So why should they have to do all the work? It's up to mums to look after their children, in every way, until they're eighteen. Mums must do all their homework, wash their clothes, make all their meals, polish their shoes, give them lots of pocket money, make them chips with every meal, including breakfast, and never give them liver or porridge and most important of all, no comic must ever be thrown out, or even touched. Are you receiving me, Sally from Palace Avenue?"

"Oh, that's very good, Ziggy. Can I have a photograph of you? Actually it's Palace Road, not Palace Avenue. Number thirteen. You won't forget to send me one?"

"I knew that. Aren't your two children called Jack and Sophie?"

"That's amazing, Ziggy. How did you know?"

"And I know the class they're in."

Through the glass partition Oz could see the producer bouncing up and down, waving through the glass, giving the thumbs up.

"I know everything," said Ziggy. "I'm not just the bestest Agony Uncle in the whole goddam world, I'm also psychic. I'm looking straight down the telephone wires now and I can see right into your head. So if you're *not* very very good to Jack and Sophie from now on, I'll find out about it.

"Next caller please."

The producer put on a pop song, then he came

through on the headphones to Oz.

"Absolutely ace, Ziggy old son! The switchboard is jammed. Fantastic. How did you know all that?"

"Easy peasy, japanese," said Oz. "I have my methods. But my throat's a bit sore. Could you manage a chocolate milk shake?"

"No problem," said the producer.

"And large french fries and a double cheeseburger . . ."

"A pleasure," said the producer. "But hold on. I'll just put through the next caller . . ."

"My name is Deirdre," said a voice on the phone, "and I'm sure you won't really be able to help me at all . . ."

"Let me be the judge of that," said Oz, but rather carefully. There was something about the voice he recognized.

"It's about my boyfriend. He's said to me, 'Trotty, we just can't keep going on like this any longer' . . ."

"Thought you said you was called Deirdre?"

"Well my full name's Deirdre Turkey and when I was little I was called Trot or Trotty. There used to be a dance called the Turkey Trot, anyway it's all a bit silly now and nothing really to do with . . ."

"Miss Turkey!"

Oz tried to hide under the table, forgetting for a moment he was in a studio all on his own and that no one could see him, certainly not his teacher.

It was a good bit of information, though, finding out her name was Deirdre, also known as Trotty. Oz made a mental note to use that some time. Against her.

"We've been going out for a long time now and I thought he was very fond of me, but suddenly he's sort of turned strange . . ."

"He's not married, is he?" asked Oz.

"How dare you!" said Miss Turkey. "Certainly not."

"Well, a lot of people I listen to on radio phone-ins, I mean that ring me up on radio phone-ins, they say that sort of thing to me all the time . . ."

"It's not like that at all. But I just don't understand it."

"Have you been telling him off?" asked Oz.

"Well," started Miss Turkey.

"You look, I mean, you sound the bossy type to me, the sort what corrects people's grammar when they're doing no harm to nobody, and tells them to wait in line and gets really upset when they make a noise and you give them detentions for nothing at all and I bet you're the sort who goes mad when you see messy handwriting . . ."

"As a matter of fact, Ziggy, that is most remarkable. It does happen to be one of my little phobias . . ."

"Have you been to the British Museum recently? You sound educated to me. I went last week with my mum, I mean with my man, my bodyguard, and I was looking at all these scribbles by that girl Shelley who lived in Wordsworth and all those other famous people and the writing was terrible, really rotten, all messy and scored out and full of stains. But they're famous now, aren't they? Right? So you stop telling other people off."

"Well, I can see your point," said Miss Turkey.

"You'd see even better if you had your hair cut. That old-fashioned fringe is really silly, always thought so, I mean since you started talking to me."

"How on earth did you . . .?"

"From now on you must *encourage* people all the time, this boyfriend of yours, if you really have one, and all the people you come across, especially any twelve-year-old boys.

"From now on, just say nice things to them. Or shut up. Next caller, please."

"It's about my dad," said a boy's voice. "He's really rotten to me sometimes."

"You're lucky to have a dad," said Oz. "I know some people who don't have no dad at all."

"Well, he's OK sometimes, but he won't let me go to London this Saturday and it's Arsenal's big match and I wanna go 'cos . . ."

"You're not called Damian, are you? Or perhaps Desmond?" said Oz. He had recognized the voice almost from the beginning.

"Who told you that?" said Dez.

The producer was waving wildly once again, throwing his hands in the air.

"Desmond, that's it. All half-witted, really stupid Arsenal supporters are called stupid names like Desmond, or Garry or Del or Bonzo . . ."

Oz was trying to remember all the Arsenal

supporters he knew, just so he could get his own back on them, all at one go.

"How did you know . . ."

"So you don't follow football then, Dessie baby."

"I do," said Desmond, "just told you."

"How can you, if you follow Arsenal."

"Ha ha ha," said Desmond.

"Watch it, son," said Oz. "I make the smart remarks on this programme.

"But I do have one piece of advice for you. From now on, follow a proper football team. Tottenham Hotspur FC.

"Next half-witted caller, please . . ."

"I'm a single parent," said a rather hesitant voice on the phone.

"Hard cheese," said Oz, very quickly, hardly listening to the caller.

He was now becoming a bit too sharp and smart. He was also just starting his milk shake and cheeseburger, so he was only half concentrating on what was being said to him.

"It's my twelve-year-old son. He just seems to be in a daydream every morning when he's supposed to be getting ready for school and it's becoming very irritating . . ."

Oz choked on his food and started spluttering.

"And he keeps on losing things," continued the voice. "His grandfather has given him so many presents over the years, but he never looks after them. Can you hear me? The line seems to have gone a bit funny . . ."

"Technical problems," said Oz, trying to disguise his voice. "I might have to cut you off . . ."

"Oh, don't do that. I liked the sound of your voice and thought you might be able to help me. I don't have many people I can tell these little things to. You sounded warm and sort of familiar. You don't live in this town, do you . . .?"

"London," muttered Oz, this time as deep as possible, making the most of his eighteen-year-old vocal chords.

"I think there might be something wrong with my phone. It was working yesterday because my son, oh now I remember, he was sitting on it, while he was having his breakfast, that's the sort of really annoying thing he . . . oh, what's happened to this line . . . what's your real name by the way? I know it can't really be Ziggy . . . You do sound ever so familiar . . ."

The woman's voice was still talking, but Oz had taken off his headphones, thrown them on the table, and was across the studio, pulling open the heavy door, almost knocking down the receptionist girl who was bringing in some more food.

"You haven't finished yet, love, have you?" she said.

"Gotta rush," said Oz. "Tell the producer. Due in London ten minutes ago. I forgot all about it. BBC TV want to give me my own prog. Bye-ee . . ."

Oz ran down the stairs, and out into the street. He didn't stop until he had reached his grandfather's flat. Being eighteen, it was surprising how fast he could run through the town.

He carefully unlocked his grandfather's front door, crept into the bedroom and hung up the magic belt in the dank and dark wardrobe, making sure he put it away exactly where he'd found it.

As soon as he closed the wardrobe door, Oz turned back into little Ossie. He was now only twelve years old again, hardly strong enough to

43

carry a big belt, never mind put it round his bird-like waist.

After tea, Ossie said he would clear up, much to his mother's surprise.

"No, you have a rest, Mum. Put your feet up on the couch."

"What a creep you are, Ossie," said Lucy.

"Just trying to be helpful. Then I'll clear up my room, tidy my clothes. I've got a list here, Mum. Just so I won't forget things."

"Who left the phone off the hook?" said Lucy. "I bet it was you, Ossie. Typical. He's always doing that, isn't he, Mum?"

"Not me," said Ossie.

"Actually, Lucy," said Mother, "it must have been me. How silly. I decided to ring up that radio station you love so much, Ossie.

"It was a phone-in advice programme and the young man's voice sounded so attractive. I just thought I'd try to get through."

"What did you want to ask, Mum?" said Lucy. "Tell me."

She went across and lay down with her mother on

the couch and put her arm round her.

"Oh, it was very silly. Just a personal question I thought I'd try. Nothing about you. Anyway, I never really got through. It was just a bit of amusement."

Ossie was sweeping the floor, noisily moving chairs to get at any dust and crumbs from tea.

"I'm not irritating you, am I, Mum?"

"No, dear, just carry on."

As Ossie went round the back of the couch, he jumped on top of his mother and Lucy, giving them each a cuddle.

"Stop it, Ossie," squealed Lucy. "You're hurting me."

"Right," said Ossie, getting up. "Can't hang around here. Got lots of jobs to do. Always gainfully occupied. In fact that's my advice to everyone . . ."

2

Ossie the Snooker Star

Ossie was on his way to Desmond's. He was very pleased to be invited out, at any time, for almost any reason, to anyone else's house, but there were a few things about going to Desmond's he didn't like.

As he walked past Flossie's house, an upstairs window opened and Flossie leaned out and waved at him. Ossie knew it was Flossie's house, knew that it was her bedroom, knew that it was her own fair, rather plump arm waving at him, but at that moment he decided to bend down and tie up the laces on his Adidas trainers. He wasn't quite sure why he did this. He blamed it on his grandad. He too often chose not to hear people or see people, if he didn't feel like hearing or seeing them. Anyway, Ossie's laces had to be done up.

"She won't let me in otherwise," said Ossie to himself. "I know her."

Desmond's mother was a stickler for such things. You had to wash your hands before you ate anything in her flat. If you sat at the table, you had to say, "Please may I get down?" when you'd finished eating. And you had to say, "Thank you, Mrs Peacock" after everything, even just a crisp or a glass of water, or else she would go on at you, giving these funny looks, and you might never get invited again.

It was only recently that Desmond had started having Ossie round to play. It had all seemed so strange at first. Desmond's home even had a different smell. Not a nasty smell. Not a particularly nice smell. Just not the smell of his mother's house.

The food at Desmond's tasted different as well, which Ossie could never quite understand. He'd always thought chips were chips, but Desmond's mother must use different oil or fat. Perhaps different potatoes. Even a tin of Heinz beans didn't seem quite the same. But they always had bottles of sauce, which Ossie's mum never allowed in her house.

Desmond lived in a large new block, twelve storeys high, with lots of corridors and wings. Ossie was always a bit nervous of the lift, in case it got stuck, or some big lads got in and started on him. He was also a bit afraid of the balconies. Looking out, even on the first floor, made him dizzy.

Desmond's was a second-floor flat, number 69, at the end of a long corridor, so it wasn't too far to walk.

Ossie said, "Hi" and grunted to a few kids he recognized from his school as he walked down the corridor. Down below, he could see others playing football, cycling round, going on skateboards.

"Lucky beggars," thought Ossie. "Dez always has people to play with. It must be trific, living in a block like this, all these things to do, not like my rotten house. I'd never be bored, if I lived here."

Ossie lived in a small, modern, semi-detached, as his mother always pointed out, but Ossie said it was like a rabbit hutch.

"Can't even swing a cat in my room," thought Ossie to himself. "I wonder why people want to swing cats? Perhaps that's how they measured rooms in the olden days. Then with big rooms they'd tie two cats together by the tail and swing them. Really big rooms you'd swing nine cats.

Probably where cat of nine tails comes from."

"Wanna play football, Ossie?" shouted a voice from below in the play area.

"No fanks. Goin a Dez's," grunted Ossie.

He always grunted and mumbled with his friends. That was what you did. It made his mother furious, if he did it at home. That was one thing about Desmond's place. No one ever corrected your grammar or your language.

The best thing about Dez's was the fact that he always had the latest and very best toys, especially electronic toys. The moment a new computer was advertised, Dez had it. The latest video equipment, you could be sure Dez would have it first.

But the bestest thing of all in Dez's house, so Ossie thought, was something which Dez had just got which was not electrical or electronic or even computer-operated. It was basically just a large lump of wood, with legs on.

"Oh, if only I had one in my house, but *she* wouldn't allow it . . ."

Ossie pressed the bell and heard it chime inside, playing a tune, like the ones on ice-cream vans.

"Wish we had a proper bell," thought Ossie.

He stood waiting. He could hear shouting inside. Dez had two big brothers, both at work. He hoped they were not at home this morning. He quite liked them, but they often wanted to play with Dez's things, which meant Dez and his friends had to wait.

"Wish I had brothers, especially big brothers. They'll always look after you. Come to school and thump your enemies. Help you mend your bike and that. I've got nobody to help me. A little sister's no use as a brother. Snot fair."

"Oh, hello, Ossie," said Mrs Peacock. Ossie immediately took off his grumpy face and smiled. He could be quite charming, when he wanted to.

"Shoes off then, please," she said, standing in front of him.

"I've just tied them up. Thought you'd want them tied up. Thought you wouldn't want me tripping and falling . . ."

"New carpet," she said proudly. "Haven't you noticed?"

Ossie pulled off his trainers, not bothering to untie the laces, and left them on the doormat. Mrs

Peacock picked them up by the laces, avoiding touching what was left of the uppers, and avoiding the dirt and grime on what was left of the soles, and deposited them in a waste-paper basket.

"And you'd better wash your hands as well," she said. "Before you start doing anything. In there, please."

Ossie did what he was told, giving his hands a quick wet in their bathroom sink, then he went into the sitting room where Dez was lying on the floor, playing with a new remote control. It not only changed channels but moved the TV set around, so you could watch it wherever you were in the room. Even from the hall or the kitchen, you could still see it. As they had three televisions anyway, it did seem to Ossie not exactly necessary, but pretty amazing all the same.

"Heh, brilliant," said Ossie. "That's mass. Really lush. Can I have a go?"

Ossie was allowed to have a go and Desmond explained how it worked. That was one thing about Dez. He did let people have a go.

"Coke, orange juice or Seven Up?"

Mrs Peacock had put her apron on and was

standing in the kitchen doorway. That was the good thing about Mrs Peacock. She was very generous with drinks and stuff.

"Coke. With lots of ice," said Ossie. "Please." He just remembered the "please" in time.

She brought him his drink and Ossie flopped down on a blue and pink striped couch to drink it, as it was now Dez's go with the remote control.

"Not there!"

Ossie almost jumped, and nearly spilt his drink.

"That's my new couch," said Mrs Peacock. "Look, go over to that little table and drink it. Do be careful, Ossie. I don't want any mess in here, right. Now I've warned you, Desmond. Or you'll get the back of my hand."

She went back into the kitchen and closed the door.

"Stupid old cow," said Dez.

Ossie was rather shocked. He would never say that about his mother. Silly, perhaps even stupid, but not an old cow.

The Big Attraction of Desmond's was the fact that he'd just got a new snooker table. They had two games. And Desmond won both easily.

Ossie couldn't quite understand it. He knew the rules better than Desmond, knew the shots that should be taken or attempted, how to slice the ball and top it and even jump over balls. It was all in his head, every move, every perfect shot.

"It's this stupid table," said Ossie. "It's not straight. You already know all the slopes, so that's why you won."

"Get lost," said Dez. "Just because you're losing!"

He sang it out, the way they do at football matches when one crowd has a go at the rival crowd.

"You're always losing anyway, being a Spurs supporter," said Desmond.

Ossie gave him a push, just a little one, but Desmond was standing with the cue between his legs and he fell over backwards. Luckily, he landed on the couch, where he lay, pretending to be injured, just putting it on.

"Desmond? You're not playing on that couch, are you?"

It was Mrs Peacock from the kitchen. Ossie could not believe it. How could she know anyone was on the couch?

Desmond jumped up quickly, which proved he wasn't hurt.

"Is the couch bugged?" said Ossie. "Has she got one-way mirrors?"

"She knows every bleeding thing," said Desmond. "She's a witch, that's what."

"Come on, anyway," said Ossie, "let's have one more game. I'll hammer you this time."

He picked up Desmond's cue from the carpet and was about to hand it to him, when he noticed it was much bigger and heavier than the one he'd been using.

"I'll have this one this time. You've had it twice."

"Give us that," said Desmond, trying to grab it. "That's my best cue. Me dad bought it for me. I can't play with any others."

"Oh yes, you let *me* play with the bad one. Look at this rubbish. It's got a bend in it and the bit on the top isn't straight. Who stuck it on?"

"Yeh, that came with the table. There's two of them. Try the other if you like."

Ossie found it under the table, but it had no tip at all.

"I'm keeping this one," said Ossie. "I'm the guest. I'll have the best cue."

Desmond slowly picked up the other cue, the bent one Ossie had been playing with, then went across to the scoreboard to put it straight, moving the pointers back to nothing, ready for the new game.

"That's another thing," said Ossie. "I'll keep the score this time, if you don't mind."

Ossie smiled. He would be bound to win this time.

He'd suspected that Desmond fiddled the score. And he'd had the best cue.

"I was just messing around those two games," said Ossie. "Getting the feel of the table. I always find it takes time to get used to a new table, to get the feel of the felt. Heh, that's good, the feel of the felt, the felt of the feel, good joke, eh, Desmond."

"You'll be the good joke," said Desmond. "When I hammer you."

"No chance," said Ossie. "I'll go first. Out of my way, peasant . . ."

If Ossie had to choose and could be brilliant at just one sport, he would choose football, but the trouble was that so far he showed few signs of his inner soccer brilliance and talent.

"But when I'm eighteen, I'll show them."

Kicking a football, he found that so hard, being small and weedy and slight. Dribbling in the playground with a plastic ball, that was OK, he was good at that, and even better with a tennis ball in the back garden, dribbling round Lucy. That was when his best and most brilliant football skill was shown.

But when they played at school, on a proper pitch, with real goal posts, real nets, real corner flags, things never seemed to go right. Bigger boys always went straight through him. If he tried to tackle, he got hurt. If he tried a long kick, it just rolled a few metres. If he took a throw in, it landed at his feet, or even worse, behind his back.

"Well, when it's wet and muddy what do you expect with a real leather ball. Snot fair. But just wait till I'm eighteen. I'll take such long throw-ins they'll be like corner kicks."

With snooker, Ossie had greater hopes. That called for finesse and touch, not brute force. He was convinced he could do all that now, without having to wait till he was eighteen.

★

Ossie managed to get a red potted after only two attempts, which was good going for him, while Desmond hadn't even got started. Then he went for a blue, and hit it well, not quite in the hole he was after, but it went whizzing round the half-sized table, straight for the far corner where it sat on the edge of the hole.

Desmond was at that moment looking at his rotten cue, cursing away, so Ossie gave the table a quick shake, pushing his feet against the rather thin legs of the table, just a slight touch, enough to tip the blue into the hole.

"Si-ix nil, six nil, si-ix nil, six nil," sang Ossie, putting up a score of eight on the board.

"I saw that," said Desmond. "Cheater."

"Mistake," said Ossie. "Sorry. Me fingers slipped."

At least Desmond had not seen him move the table.

Ossie completely missed the next red, hitting a green by mistake, so he lost four points, but he wasn't too worried.

"I'm really getting the hang of this now," he said. "Not a bad table you've got here, Dez, old son.

Mind you, I prefer slate myself. That's what I'm used to. These hardboard tables take some playing on. Skill people like me need the best surface . . ."

"Oh, shurrup, you," said Desmond. "You're putting me off."

Desmond took his shot at last, and got a red in, then went on to get the green. He managed another red, then he got a black down as well.

"What a fluke," said Ossie.

"The score," said Desmond. "Put it up. Don't cheat."

Ossie wasted his next three chances, while Desmond got further ahead. The better cue had at first made a slight difference, but now Ossie was playing much as he always played. Balls were refusing to go in the direction he sent them, no matter how carefully he aimed.

"It's me fingers," said Ossie. "You're OK. You've got fat fingers. I've got little weedy fingers. I can't get a proper grip. Snot fair."

He wasted another chance. Desmond had by now got all the reds in and was slowly picking off the colours, getting first the yellow and then the green.

At last Ossie got one down, the brown, and

turned to aim at the pink, which was very near him, easy peasy right over a hole.

"The blue's next," said Desmond.

"No, it's not," said Ossie.

"I thought you could play this game. What a dum dum. Knew you were a liar, Ossie Osgood. Always knew it."

"New rules," said Ossie. "You *can* go for the blue, but you don't have to . . ."

"Mum!" shouted Desmond. "It's blue isn't it, not pink?"

"If you are on that couch," shouted his mother, "I'll come through there and belt both of you."

"See, now look what you've done," said Desmond.

"OK, have it your own way," said Ossie, turning round to look for the blue. It was stuck out in the middle of the table.

"I'll need the rest. Where is it? Hope you've got one. Call this a snooker table. Huh. Just a toy. You should see me on a real table."

Desmond got the rest from under the table and handed it to Ossie.

As Ossie leaned on the table, almost lying on it to

60

get a good position, Desmond pulled back his legs.

"Not allowed," said Desmond. "One foot on the floor at least."

"Don't be stupid," said Ossie. "I can't reach the rotten ball."

"That's your fault," said Desmond. "Titch."

"And anyway this rest is useless. How are you supposed to hold it and do a shot."

"Oh, so you don't know how to use the rest either. Thought you could play this game. You're too small, that's your trouble."

"I can't help that, can I."

It was true. Ossie's little hands were not up to using the rest, and his legs were too short to let him lean across the table.

He missed the blue completely, giving away another five points. Desmond, who was at least three inches taller, picked up the rest, and got the blue down, and then the pink.

As he was lining himself up for the black, Ossie began to fiddle with the table legs, hoping to put Desmond off by making the table wobble, but Desmond got the black down and won the game, fifty-two to five.

Suddenly the table collapsed, falling on top of Ossie, trapping him underneath, his arms and legs getting caught up in the struts and bars as the table went to pieces on top of him.

"Serves you right," said Desmond. "You're useless."

Ossie eventually got himself up, then said he had to go. He didn't even thank Mrs Peacock for all her drinks and stuff.

"If only I wasn't so small," he thought as he walked home, "I'd show them all."

Ossie had expected to spend the whole day at Desmond's, as he'd also been invited to stay and have lunch, but with Desmond being so rotten to him, showing off and being flash and all that, the day had finished earlier than he had expected. He couldn't go home, because Lucy and Mum, taking advantage of his absence, had gone out for the day shopping.

"I'll have some egg and bacon at Grandad's," thought Ossie. "He always has egg and bacon. He never shows off, not like that Desmond. Thinks he's it, just 'cos he's an inch bigger than me."

Ossie kicked an empty beer can along the gutter. "OK, two inches bigger."

With a final kick, he sent the can into someone's front door.

"I know *he* says three inches. But he always cheats on every score . . ."

On his way to Grandad's, Ossie came to a huge queue. It appeared to have no beginning and no end. He followed it the way it seemed to be going, round and round a block, and eventually came to a large brightly lit building he had never seen before, all flashing lights and chromium. Two massive blokes in evening suits and purple shirts were at the entrance, letting the queue in, one by one.

Ossie had to move backwards into the road before he could look up and make out the flashing letters above. "SNOOKERAMA."

There were lots of posters round the entrance hall announcing that World Champion Steve Davis would be giving a demonstration match, today, in the famous Snookerama.

Ossie tried to get closer, just to see how much it cost, but the crowd was too dense. He got down on his knees and worked his way between the legs, trying to reach the other side of the queue and read the posters properly.

"What the hell are you doing, son?"

Ossie felt himself going up in the air, as if he'd been picked up by one of those giant hands you see in fun fairs, which grab a present, if you're lucky. It *was* a giant hand, belonging to one of the doormen in evening dress.

Ossie was looking straight into his droopy moustache. Close up, he could see that there were bits of food in it. He also noticed that the man's shirt collar was dirty, his bow tie was made of shiny plastic and his left ear was like a forest. The man had not had a very good shave that morning either. But his strength was real enough. So was his bad temper.

"You have to be eighteen, right," roared the man. "These are licensed premises, right. Don't let me see you crawling on my pavement again."

He then let Ossie drop.

Ossie lay for a bit, getting his breath back, checking no bones were broken. Then slowly he got up, muttering to himself.

"You big ape," said Ossie. But ever so softly.

"Egg and bacon is off," so Grandad announced. "But sausage and bacon is on. You can even do yourself some fried bread, in special dripping, and there might be a couple of tomatoes."

Ossie stood thinking for a long time. He was starving.

"And perhaps a bit of black pudding, if you're good."

Ossie knew that was a special treat. His grandfather got it sent from the North and usually did not let anybody else have any of it.

"You can go and borrow an egg from old Ma Pigg," said Grandad, "if you're really desperate."

"No, thanks," said Ossie.

"You been drinking that horrible Coko stuff?" asked his grandfather. "Ruins your appetite."

"No, it's just, well I've got to go somewhere and I haven't really got much time. Got jobs to do for Mum. Just wanted to pop in and see how you are."

"Well," said Grandad.

"How are you then?" asked Ossie.

"No better for seeing you. Don't know why you

66

come, I'm sure. Close the door when you go out."

Ossie went back down the little hall, opened the door and listened.

"Modern generation," he could hear his grandfather saying. "Too lazy to make their own snacks. When I was his age . . ."

Ossie sneaked into the bedroom. Very quickly he went into the wardrobe and put on the magic belt, remembering just in time to close his eyes and wish very, very hard that he was eighteen.

"Take us in, Mister," said a little boyish voice.

Oz was just about to go into the Snookerama. Being eighteen and ever so big and strong, he had just walked to the top of the queue. Nobody had dared to push him out of the way or object. He was pretending anyway to be a guard, muttering "Security" as he pushed past people, flashing a card he had found in his pocket.

"Mister, take us with you, please."

Oz looked down from his great height, and saw that it was Desmond and two other boys from his class.

"No chance," said Oz. "You don't even look

eight, never mind eighteen. They don't allow babies in here."

"Oh, please," said Dez.

The two bouncers in evening dress were busy further down the queue, keeping everyone in line. When Oz came up to them, from behind, they thought he had come out of the hall itself.

"Look, you two apes," said Oz, "I thought you'd been given orders not to let any kids in. You know what Steve's like. Any problems, any hassles, that's it."

"You wif Steve Davis?" asked one of the purple-shirted bouncers.

"S'right," said Oz. "Private bodyguard."

Oz flashed his card. The purple shirt lumbered across to pick up Dez. Oz could see that he was really rather fat, not at all muscular, with a large beer belly.

"No need for that, Fatso," said Oz.

With one hand, Oz grabbed the bouncer by the scruff of his collar. He was amazed that it was so easy, but then he was eighteen and very fit and very strong. He even got him a few inches off the ground.

"Just cool it, man, cool it," said Oz.

"Wasn't gonna hurt him," spluttered the bouncer.

"Just remember," said Oz. "Today's kids are tomorrow's customers. All right?"

Inside the hall, there were about twenty snooker tables, all full-sized, with special arc lights over each of them, like searchlights. It made the rest of the hall seem rather dark and it took Oz some time to adjust his vision.

It was very crowded, but Oz found that if you walked round as if you owned the place, as if you owned the whole world, then people got out of your way. No need to push or shove. A strong presence seemed to be enough.

"Ladies and gentlemen, Steve Davis is now going to play one last game."

The words came from a little platform where a self-important man in a white jacket was at a microphone. The hall went quiet.

"Steve would like one volunteer to come forward, one of our newer, younger members, not anyone who has played so far this afternoon, or any of the Committee." He paused. "In other words, not one of our resident experts."

There was polite laughter. Oz looked around. There seemed to be no volunteers. Before he really knew what he was doing, he had pushed himself to the front and was standing in the bright lights, right beside Steve Davis.

"A big hand for this young gentleman," said the announcer. "What's your name, young man?"

"Oz."

"I didn't ask where you were from," said the announcer, laughing at his own joke. "So you're from Australia, are you?"

"No," said Oz, "but I got an aunty living there. I've never been, but she once sent me a toy kangaroo which I often sleep with, I mean used to sleep with, when I was . . . ."

"Fantastic," said the announcer, "really fantastic," but with no real enthusiasm. He was looking at Oz carefully, wondering if perhaps they had made a mistake in letting an ordinary person come forward.

"Well then, ladies and gentlemen, I have to tell you that for this final display, I mean very competitive match against our young Australian friend here, Steve is going to give him a twenty-point lead. A big hand for both of them, ladies and gentlemen, please."

Oz stood beside Steve Davis. They shook hands with each other and then another man came forward, also in evening dress, wearing white gloves.

"Looks a very clean hall," said Oz. "Why's he got gloves on? He's worse than Mrs Peacock."

"Who?" asked Steve Davis, smiling kindly at Oz, but not really listening to his mumbles.

"Oh, she's really stupid. She's the sort who likes you to put gloves on just to go to the toilet."

Steve Davis smiled wearily.

"I'll break," he said. "If you don't mind."

"My pleasure, Steve," said Oz. "You probably need all the practice you can get."

"Ladies and gentlemen," said the announcer. "Let's have best of order and complete quiet. Thank you very much."

All the lights in the hall were dimmed and every eye focused on Oz and Steve Davis.

Steve Davis had deliberately broken to give Oz the best possible chance, scattering the balls all round the table, leaving them in fairly easy positions, all neatly spread out.

Then he stepped back, allowing Oz to have his first go.

Oz chose a cue from a long rack. It seemed very heavy, not the sort of cue he had ever played with, but he could tell it was a very good one, the sort professionals use.

With his first stroke, Oz missed the ball completely.

He was surprised by the weight of the cue, the intensity of the lights and the size of the table, which seemed to stretch out miles ahead of him, almost as big as a football pitch.

"Just testing," said Oz quickly, pretending he had meant it. As he hadn't hit the cue ball, it was still his go.

"Not used to full size," said Oz. "Or real slate. Dez only has a hardboard table."

Oz took careful aim. His left hand was beginning to feel more comfortable on the table, solid and strong, making a perfect arch for his cue to rest on. There was no shaking or slipping. It wasn't like holding an inferior cue, on an inferior table, with weedy, inferior hands. His right arm also felt comfortable, steady yet gentle.

He had watched Steve Davis on the television enough times, and knew what was *supposed* to happen, but it was only now, when he was the same height, that he felt in complete control.

The noise of Oz's cue hitting the ball was solid and sharp, almost like gunfire, not that thin, slippery, slidery, bangy sort of noise you get on toy tables with toy-like cues.

A red ball went straight in. Steve Davis nodded his head. He motioned with his eyes towards the black. Oz thought why not. Looks quite easy.

The black went straight in. Oz could hardly believe it. Several people round the hall gave him a clap.

There was a red almost in a pocket, so he aimed for that, without looking at Steve Davis. That went down as well. The score went up on the electric board for all to see: twenty-nine to Oz, nil to Steve Davis. Oz had, of course, been given a start.

"Try the pink," said Steve Davis, softly, so that no one else could hear. "Not too much bottom."

"Don't be rude," said Oz, thinking Steve was

being personal. Now that he was eighteen, he did have a rather large posterior. As a twelve-year-old, he had no bottom at all. Then he realized it was technical advice. So he took it, putting the pink straight in.

In hardly any time at all, Oz had cleared four reds, one after the other, and three colours, without Steve Davis even starting. There was a tremendous roar from the crowd. Everyone was applauding Oz. It had looked like good luck at first, a few fortunate bounces and in-offs, but now the crowd realized that they were watching a very confident, very talented, if rather unorthodox player.

The score was forty-five to nil, when at last he missed a colour.

"That's the best break I've ever made," said Oz, standing back from the table. "Well, I did once get forty-six, but that was when I was doing the score, and playing on my own, and no one was watching, and it was on Dez's little baby table . . ."

Steve Davis was now in action. He was into a break of forty, scarcely appearing to look at the balls.

Oz was sitting down, drinking a glass of water,

looking into space, turning his face this way and that, ignoring the audience who were leaning forward, right behind him.

He had thought about standing and watching the world champion at work, but on television he'd noticed the players always sat down and went into a sort of daydream. Oz was trying his best to look like a professional, closing his eyes as if meditating.

There was a loud "Oooh" from the crowd, which startled Oz from his thoughts. Steve Davis had missed a red. He'd stuck at forty-three. Or had he done it deliberately?

The red had been left in a much easier position, so Oz had no trouble getting it down. He then finished off the final reds, plus two colours, which brought his score to sixty-seven. The crowd had now gone silent, wondering if perhaps a future world champion was performing before them. It was now all on the colours.

Oz went for the yellow, taking aim very carefully, not because he didn't think he'd make it, but because a horrible thought had just struck him.

"Is it the green or the brown next?" thought Oz to himself. "Oh no, don't say I've forgotten. Now what did Dez tell me. I can't show myself up by having to ask Steve . . ."

Oz stood back from the table, thinking hard. The audience was quiet. Was this new superstar-in-the-making about to collapse? Had the strain been too great for him? Was it luck after all?

"Er, Steve," said Oz slowly. "Watcha think? The green, hmm?"

Oz tried to phrase it as vaguely as possible, not admitting he didn't know which ball you were supposed to go for.

"Yes, that is the green," said Steve. "But get the yellow first."

The yellow was in a very difficult position, but Oz simply let fly and did his best shot of the whole game. The yellow went straight down.

To Oz's amazement, Steve Davis stepped forward and shook his hand.

"There's only twenty-five left on the table," said Steve. "I can't beat you now. You've won. Congratulations."

Up on the electric scoreboard, Oz could see the result. Oz 69: Steve Davis 43.

There was a tremendous roar from the crowd and everyone rushed forward to congratulate Oz. The bouncer with the droopy moustache was almost first forward, thrusting an autograph book into Steve Davis's face.

"It's been a pleasure meeting you," said Steve to Oz.

The bouncer looked at Steve Davis. Then at Oz.

"Heh, doesn't he work for you? I did think it was a fiddle, having one of your staff planted in the audience to play the last game . . . Can I see your pass, please . . ."

"Er, I've got to go now," said Oz. "Thanks for the game, Steve."

Oz disappeared into the crowd as fast as he could. Most people wanted to get near Steve Davis, so Oz was able to push his way through.

He ran out into the street and headed for his grandad's house, as fast as his strong, muscular legs could take him.

"About Christmas," said his mother.

"Yes," said Ossie, who was having his tea, watching the last bit of chocolate cake, just in case

Lucy snatched it. He was starving.

"Are you listening, Ossie? I thought you had lunch at Desmond's today."

"Christmas, yes, I can hear you," replied Ossie. "Comes round every year. In December usually. If you take that chocolate cake, Lucy . . ."

"We've been round all the shops today and I'm thinking of a very special present for you. It's going to be very expensive, so it may have to count as your birthday present as well. Would you mind?"

"Don't mind, Mum, whatever you think."

"It is a problem, though," said his mother, looking round the room, half talking to herself. "I don't know where it will go. They do take up so much space, even the smaller ones . . ."

"If it's a snooker table, Mum," said Ossie, "forget it."

"What?" said his mother. "Who said anything about a snooker table?"

She looked at Lucy, as if to say she must have been telling tales. Lucy shook her head.

"I played at Desmond's today," said Ossie. "Hammered him of course, I always do. He's useless. Not strong enough to even hit the balls properly. But the thing is, I've decided I don't want a snooker table any more. Unless you get a full-sized one, made of slate, a real one. What's the point? When you're as good as me, only the very best will do, the real professional ones."

"But I thought it was what you most wanted in your whole life," said his mother. "That's what you told me last week."

"Did I?" said Ossie. "That was ages ago, long before I, er, knew much about real snooker.

"Save your money, Mum. I've now decided that I can wait. Till I'm eighteen, or so . . ."

3

Ossie the Ace Reporter

Mr Bott had called a meeting of the whole first year to tell them some "exciting news". That was how the notice on the first year board in the main hall had described it.

"Would have been *really* exciting if he'd called it during lessons," said Ossie.

"So we could have missed Maths," said Desmond.

"Yeh," said Ossie. "Or French."

"Or English," said Desmond.

"Oh, I quite like English," said Ossie.

"That's interesting," said Dez, "considering how useless you are at it."

They went down the corridor, hitting each other with their sports bags. At the same time, they were pushed and jostled by bigger boys and girls, all going in the opposite direction.

Ossie and Dez had had their lunch, but instead of going straight out to play football in the playground, they had decided to give Old Botty a few minutes of their valuable time, just in case he really had something exciting to say to the first year.

"Praps they're going on strike again," said Dez. "That would be brill. Really lush."

"Hope not," said Ossie. "Rather be in this rotten old school than hanging around rotten old home."

Ossie liked school, quite a lot, but he wasn't going to say so. Dez would just get it all wrong and smirk and bring it up at the wrong moment, such as the next time Ossie said he hated school.

"School is meant to be a place where you broaden your horizons," Mr Bott was saying.

"You mean broaden your bum," whispered Dez. He and Ossie started to giggle.

"So much of your school time is spent learning," said Mr Bott, "picking up knowledge in order to pass examinations which the State decrees you must do in order to go out into the world and get proper jobs, though I have to admit with the state the country is in at the moment . . ."

"Oh, get on with it," whispered Ossie. "What a lot of crud."

"I'm giving him one more minute," said Dez, "then I'm off."

". . . so what I am proposing is an enterprise in which every one of you can join, regardless of your academic skills. Who knows, some of you sitting here today might well discover talents which you never suspected you had." Mr Bott paused for effect. "Or we never suspected."

Only about twenty of the first years had actually turned up, but Mr Bott was going on as if he was addressing the Albert Hall, or Wembley Stadium. One or two girls were already sneaking out at the back of the hall.

"We are going to begin a first year magazine," announced Mr Bott, waiting for rapturous applause. Instead, a few more people left.

"I am willing to give you some of my free time to get it launched. I did do quite a bit of student journalism, when I was at varsity, and was quite good at it, though I say so myself . . ."

"No one else will," whispered Dez, starting to get up.

"Heh, it sounds quite good," said Ossie. "Don't go now. Let's hang on a bit, Dez."

In Ossie's mind, he could already see himself as editor, telling people to hold the front page, starting crusades, launching campaigns, exposing villains.

"And there's a lot of real villains in this school," thought Ossie. "Whoever took my locker key, that's one for a start."

Mr Bott went on to explain that the first year magazine would be an experiment. There was of course the School Magazine, which would still go on. "As you know, that's mainly run by the sixth form, properly printed and a jolly good production, though one day we might rival it. Har, har, har.

"We will be printing our new magazine in the media resources room. What am I saying? *You* will be printing it. Once I have got you started, I want you to do it, all on our own. Writing everything. Doing the cartoons and drawings. Laying out the pages, marking up the copy, pasting up the proofs, printing and stapling, perhaps getting advertising, designing posters, organizing distribution, doing the selling, then collecting the money and doing the accounts.

"So you can see, boys and girls, there is scope for each one of you, no matter what your talents are. This might, you never know, take you in a completely new direction and give you a passion, nay, an occupation for life . . ."

"I've already got that," whispered a girl near Ossie, and all her friends started giggling. Ossie shussed them to be quiet.

Ossie was very interested in the whole project. Personally, he would like to have a go at everything. He and Lucy, years ago, had tried their own little magazine, which contained a serial story and was to run and run for years, but only one edition had come out. Nearly. Well, they did finish the first page . . .

"We need a title first," said Mr Bott. "Any suggestions?"

"Botty's Bum," said Dez. No one giggled at this. It was just too silly.

"The *Brookfield Express*," said Flossie Teacake, putting up her hand and shouting out.

"Jolly good idea," said Mr Bott.

"The *Brookfield Guardian*," said another girl.

"The *Brookfield Sun*," said a boy, "then we can

have pin-ups of the teachers on page three."

Everyone laughed at this, even Mr Bott, though it was a strain. His face was not accustomed to laughter.

"How about the *Brookfield Bugle*?" said Flossie. "I don't know a newspaper or magazine called that, so it could be different."

"I like the alliteration, Flossie," said Mr Bott.

Everyone went, "Oooh!" "Big words, Mr Bott!" "You what?" "Whatsheonabout?"

"And I think the editor should be . . ." said Mr Bott, looking round the assembled throng, now no more than sixteen strong. He slowly went from face to face, estimating the talents and capabilities of those present.

He kept on avoiding Ossie's eye, so Ossie thought, despite the fact that Ossie strained in his seat and looked eager. Being so small and weedy, he found this very difficult.

"For the first issue, to see how it goes, I think, yes I think Flossie Teacake will be the editor. Come out here please, Flossie."

"Lucky beggar," said Ossie.

"What a creep," said Dez. "I'm not working with

her. She's bossy enough as it is."

"Now we come to sports editor," continued Mr Bott.

This time Ossie could feel himself shaking. He was a natural for that, the complete all-rounder. He might not be in any of the school teams, but that was teachers' favouritism, not his fault. He did happen to know an awful lot about every sport, from skiing to swimming, from snooker to soccer. He was surprised he had never been asked to appear on "Mastermind", answering questions on sport. Every week he knew all the answers in *Shoot*.

"Desmond Peacock," said Mr Bott. "Could you come out, please."

"I thought you were leaving," said Ossie, trying to hold him back, but Dez jumped up, pushed Ossie away, and went up to the front.

In turn, two assistant editors were appointed, a features editor, a film reviewer, a photographer, a woman's editor, though that took some time as three girls protested about the title "woman's editor". There were shouts of "sexist" and Mr Bott was forced to re-word it. It was turned into fashion editor. The chosen person, Sophie, would look at fashions for both boys and girls. Someone said that was ageist, so it was agreed it would cover fashions for all people of all ages.

Someone was put in charge of all the artwork, in this case a boy who was very good at drawing. Ossie went along with that. He could be a bit messy, he did admit. A printing supervisor was agreed on, and someone to be in charge of distribution, to make sure that salespeople were appointed in each of the seven classes in the first year.

Only Ossie was left, overlooked, jobless, forgotten.

"Now let me see," said Mr Bott, as if he had only just noticed that Ossie was there, that he existed, that he was on the planet.

"Stapling is a frightfully important job," he began, "which is one reason why I have left it to the end . . ."

"Liar," said Ossie to himself. "You forgot all about me."

"I think I will put you in charge of stapling," said Mr Bott, grinning for once and looking inane, so Ossie thought. "That's, of course, if you're strong enough."

★

Ossie set off to walk home on his own. He had refused to wait for Flossie Teacake, though she had asked him.

She was in a huddle anyway, by the school gate, with a lot of other kids gathered round her. Ossie decided to ignore them all.

"I've got a green eyeshade as well," he muttered to himself. "That one Grandad's got. I should have been editor, not that fat slob. Snot fair.

"As for that berk Desmond, what does he know about sport? He's alliterate."

"Hi, Grandad," said Ossie, but not nearly as loudly or as enthusiastically as usual.

He let himself into the flat, went into Grandad's little kitchen and put on the kettle, sullenly and slowly.

"What's got your rag?" asked Grandad.

"It's the school rag," said Ossie. "We're starting one, but they won't let me join in."

Ossie told his grandad everything that had happened.

"I'd have nothing to do with them," said Grandad. "Let them stick."

"I know what Mum will say," said Ossie, putting on a high voice. "'Do the stapling job, Ossie, as well as you can, and when they see how keen you are, you will be put in charge of something better.' Like the stupid old printing. I know her. Well, I'm not."

"I've got my own problems," said Grandad. "The Council has decided to repaint everything."

"That sounds good, Grandad. This place could do with brightening up."

"You should see the colour. Sort of horrible khaki green. Every door the bleedin' same. Like being in the army."

"I thought you loved the army, Grandad. You're always going on about it."

"This is different. Don't want to live in a barracks all my life."

"Can't you protest?" said Ossie.

Grandad put his finger to his lips and shook his head.

"Never draw attention to yourself. Just keep your head down. People are watching, you know. They get your number, then whoosh, you're a marked man. You can't win. But Old Ma Pigg says she's going to fettle them."

Ossie was always surprised that Grandad called her Old Ma, when he himself was so old. They both seemed ancient to him. But perhaps Old Ma Pigg was even older.

"What's she going to do then, Grandad?" said Ossie, helping himself to three of Grandad's digestive biscuits, from his private digestive biscuit tin.

"She says she's going to paint her whole flat red, white and blue. You know she loves the Royal Family. Potty, if you ask me. She'll never do it anyway. She's all talk. All those things she says she did as a girl, chaining herself to railings when she was a Sausagette . . ."

"Suffragette," said Ossie. "We did them in history. They wanted votes for women."

"Barm pot," said Grandad, "the lot of them."

As Ossie left his grandfather's block, he noticed old Mrs Pigg coming home.

She seemed much more worn than usual, all crouched and bent. She'd probably been shopping, by the look of her.

Ossie didn't believe in saying "hello" to adults, unless spoken to, and even then he allowed out only a few grunts. But this time he stopped and stared at her.

Behind Mrs Pigg was a white line, which stretched away into the distance towards the park. It appeared to be growing, the closer she trundled towards him.

"I wonder if she's leaking," thought Ossie. "Perhaps she's got a wooden leg which is full of emulsion. Grandad always says she's a barm pot."

Mrs Pigg got nearer and Ossie could see she was pushing something. It looked like a wickerwork trolley at first, the sort old people use to go shopping. He stood to the side, to let her get into the gateway to the Sheltered Housing block.

"It's one of those machines they use in the park," thought Ossie. "The thing that makes white lines for the football pitch. She must have gone and pinched it. Wait till the Parkies find out."

Mrs Pigg stood in the middle of the little lawn, a communal strip of grass for all the elderly people. It was right outside Mrs Pigg's own flat, and she always maintained it really belonged to her.

She was looking around, as if measuring the lawn with her eye. She got her breath back and heaved

the lining machine to a far corner. She then started to mark out a huge square, working her way round, enclosing the entire lawn.

"Er, do you want any help, Mrs Pigg?" said Ossie.

"Out of the way, child," she said.

"What you doing anyway?" asked Ossie.

"None of your business."

She came to a halt at a corner, trying very carefully to steer the machine in a complete right angle, but it had stuck on the verge, one wheel hanging over onto a little rose garden.

Ossie ran to help her, and this time she allowed him, but he found he couldn't move the machine.

"What a weakling," she said, very irritably. "You should be in bed, child. Oh, get out of the way. I'll do it all on my own."

She gave Ossie a push, and he realized she was quite strong after all, stronger than he was.

"Most people are," thought Ossie. "Even old-age pensioners can push me around. Snot fair. Just wait till I'm eighteen. I'll show everyone. If I ever get there."

Mrs Pigg gave one enormous pull, bending her

shoulders, and got the machine righted. Very slowly, she continued on her way.

When she'd finished marking out the square to her satisfaction, she then made two diagonal lines, from corner to corner.

"Yes, what are you staring at, child?" she said, suddenly turning on Ossie. "Get yourself off home. And don't you dare tell anyone what I'm doing. Or I'll report you to your grandfather, though he's a stupid old man and never has any idea what's going on."

"So she does know me," thought Ossie. All these times he had not been talking to her, as they passed in the hallway, he had assumed he must be invisible.

He turned to walk home, but then stopped to look back. Mrs Pigg was now in her kitchen, holding up what seemed to be an aerosol can, the sort that football hooligans use.

"Now what on earth is she doing?"

Mrs Pigg stared towards Ossie and waved a fist at him. Or she might just have been shaking the can. It was enough to make Ossie turn round and run home.

★

After tea was over, Ossie told his mother and Lucy all about the *Brookfield Bugle*, how they'd been horrible to him, carved him up, been really nasty to him, and how Old Botty had given out all the best jobs to his favourites.

Ossie's mother very quietly and calmly told Ossie that he should stick in at the stapling, do it properly, and maybe Mr Bott would realize what a treasure he had, what a good worker . . .

"I knew you'd say that," snarled Ossie. "You never take my side. Nobody ever does. Now you've given me a headache."

"Oh, who's in a bad temper tonight," said Lucy. "Little Ossie's got a little headache, eh. Oh, the poor babba!"

Ossie tried to give her a sly kick, but she moved away quickly, making faces at him, standing near her mother, so that Ossie couldn't get hold of her.

"Shall I clear the table, Mummy?" said Lucy, putting on her best soppy voice. "Ossie will just break everything. You know him."

Ossie threw himself down on the couch. Then just as suddenly he jumped up again.

"You're right, Mum," he said, all sweetness and

light. "I will try hard and do the stapling and maybe Mr Bott will eventually give me a good job. Fact I think I'll go now and do some practice stapling . . ."

"Now?" said Mrs Osgood.

"Thought you'd got a sore head," said Lucy.

"Feels a bit better," said Ossie.

"Went very quickly," said Lucy.

"It'll be starting tonight and I want to be there, you know, just to see the white lines, I mean the designs for the *Bugle* in the art room. Won't be late, Mum. Bye."

He gave his mother a little hug, which rather surprised her, after all that shouting she'd had to put up with. Ossie even smiled at Lucy as he went out of the door.

"What a funny boy," said Mrs Osgood.

"He's a barm pot, if you ask me," said Lucy. They both smiled and got on with clearing up the tea things.

Ossie could hardly believe his eyes. In just an hour, Old Ma Pigg had completely painted the lawn, filling in the shapes in the white square with red paint and blue paint. It was only when Ossie stood back that he realized she had created a gigantic Union Jack.

She had also painted red, white and blue stripes over every door, completely obliterating the Council's khaki green. She was now just finishing off the external walls on the ground floor, painting them, too, in red, white and blue.

It was getting dark, and most people had their curtains closed, so the residents were not aware of what had happened. They tended to ignore Mrs Pigg anyway. Just as she ignored little kids like Ossie.

"I bet she wouldn't ignore a Big Boy," thought Ossie, "such as a Real Reporter . . ."

He ran quickly into the main door, without Mrs Pigg seeing him. He let himself into his grandad's flat, then crept into his bedroom. The magic belt was there, left from before. Ossie quickly put it on, closed his eyes, and wished desperately to be eighteen. Once again, the magic powers took over his body.

On the way out, Oz remembered to grab the green eyeshade and an old army issue notebook.

★

"Excuse me, Madam," said Oz, pushing his green shade slightly to the back of his head, just so that he could see properly.

"Yes?" said Mrs Pigg, ever so sweetly. She was standing on some steps, finishing her final strokes. She came down the steps, beaming in satisfaction, very proud of all her handiwork.

"I'm a reporter," said Oz, wishing he'd remembered to put on that old raincoat of Grandad's. In all the films he'd ever seen, reporters always wore raincoats. "I'm from the *Bugle*. The *Brookfield Bugle*."

"Just the man I wanted," said Mrs Pigg. "Have you got shorthand?"

"Well, me legs are a big short," said Oz, forgetting for a moment he was eighteen, "but me grandad gives me exercises, swinging on a coat-hanger. He says they won't be short for ever, but I think me hands are OK . . ."

"Then get out your notebook at once."

Oz got out his notebook and tried to look as important and professional as possible.

"My name is Peggy Pigg and I'm seventy-nine and I have this statement to make," said Mrs Pigg.

She was reciting at dictation speed, which made it easy for Oz to get it all down.

"This is the first blow to be struck by the Old Age Pensioners' Liberation Army. We are sick and tired of being pushed around by the Council, by local authorities, governments, park-keepers, teenagers, hooligans, Post Office officials and owners of transistor radios. We will not put up with these sort of people any more. Right, read that back to me, please."

Luckily, she had been speaking slowly, so Oz had managed to get most of it right, though he found it hard to read his own handwriting.

"This country has gone completely to the dogs and if it was not for the Royal Family I would personally emigrate at once. They are the sole rays of hope in a very dark world. Have you got that?

"I'd like you also to send a message through your columns to the Queen Mother. My army and I wish her to be our Generalissimo. Can you spell that? We are inviting her to take the march past when we assemble tomorrow on this square, which this evening I have painted in Her Majesty's honour. All right?"

"Yes," said Oz. "Got it all down. But tell me, Madam, how many have you got in your Old Age Pensioners' Liberation Army?"

Mrs Pigg stopped and thought for a moment.

"I've got to liberate *them* first, haven't I? Some of these senior citizens are frankly pretty senile. But I intend to campaign on their behalf, then we will all arise and shake off our yokes . . ."

"Yolks?" said Oz. "My grandad loves the yolks best. He's not going to throw them away . . ."

But Mrs Pigg was not listening.

"And I have this message for the Prime Minister," said Mrs Pigg, standing now on the lower steps of her ladder, declaiming to an imaginary crowd.

"The nation's senior citizens cannot be pushed around any longer. The elderly are fighting back. Down with Ageism! Up with Pensions! All geriatric hospitals will be liberated when the revolution comes. Old Folks' Homes will be freed. All TV licences will be free. Only old people will be allowed on public buses. The Archers will be on all day long from now on . . ."

"Yes, but how many members have you got at present?" asked Oz again, sucking his pencil.

"My Chief of Staff is General Osgood. He won many medals in the last war. I have seen them myself. I have utter confidence in General Osgood's courage and character. But I would advise you not to disturb him at present, as he does go to bed rather early. He is eighty years old . . ."

Oz's pencil paused. Had she got this fact right? He had always been led to believe that Old Ma Pigg was older than Grandad; hence she was always called Old Ma. As a trained reporter, Oz would need to get everything correct, or he would have to check with his sources.

"Here, you two, what's going on?"

It was Mr Collander, the caretaker, looking very angry.

"Who's done all this? Oh my God, what a mess."

"It is *not* a mess," said Mrs Pigg, "it is a symbol of the oppressed mass of pensioners in this country who are very soon going to rise up. You shall see."

With that, Mrs Pigg got down from the steps and walked towards her flat, looking very pleased with herself.

"Oh, about a photographer," she said, turning to

Oz. "You will get one, won't you?"

"Oh, yeh. Dez has got one, instamatic, don't worry . . ."

"Come back, you," shouted the caretaker at Mrs Pigg. "I know your tricks. You're just a vandal, bleedin' vandal. You're worse than the teenagers. Spraying your stupid slogans all over the place. I've warned you already. This has gone on long enough. I'm going to report you right away to the Council."

Oz was taking down every word which the caretaker shouted at Mrs Pigg, as a good reporter should. When the caretaker went back into his own quarters to phone the Council, Oz ran off, in the direction of Brookfield School.

The story almost wrote itself. Oz hardly had to pause. He sat at the big electronic typewriter in the media resources room, which to his amazement he found he could use perfectly easily.

"When you're eighteen, and you're a real reporter, you know all about these things."

There were several first years already in the room, such as Flossie, Sophie and a few others, but he pushed them aside, saying he had an important story to write, very confidential.

"You sixth form?" Flossie asked.

"Could be," said Oz.

"What you wearing that big belt for?"

"I am rather busy. Can't you just get on with your stapling?"

"You writing your magazine? Well, ours will be much better, so there . . ."

"Get out, you kids. You don't know a thing about *real* newspapers."

One of the teachers did come in at one stage, but just ignored Oz, going off into the gym to watch the First Eleven training.

In the main hall, Oz could hear the school play being rehearsed. As usual in the evenings, there was a lot going on. But Oz was too busy with his world scoop to be disturbed by any noises.

When he'd finished, he read it through and made a few corrections. He decided, after all, not to put in the age of General Osgood. That was the only point he wasn't sure about.

He went into a little office, in the corner of the media resources room, where Mr Bott usually sat, and picked up the phone.

"Give me Fleet Street," he barked into it. Nothing happened.

He then remembered that you needed to press 9 to phone outside the school. He'd seen one of the school secretaries do that.

Still nothing happened. He thought about dialling 999, but that would get the police. Mr Collander was probably ringing them this very moment. Then he dialled 100, and eventually someone answered. He asked for Fleet Street, and was told by a very short-tempered operator to dial Directory Enquiries. He found the number at the front of a little local directory, sitting on Mr Bott's desk.

"Eh, can I have the phone number for the *Daily Express*, Fleet Street, love," said Oz, pulling down his green eyeshade, imagining he was in a TV drama. "That's London, my darling."

"I know," said the voice.

"Oh, and also gimme the *Guardian*. Thanks, sweetheart. Have a good night. Don't do anything I wouldn't do . . ."

Oz paused for a while. He now had the numbers,

but what if they each told him to go away and not be silly? But why should they? He had a very good story, full of quotes and facts. It was a pity, though, about Grandad's age. Should he ring him up and ask him? But Grandad never revealed such things, least of all to anyone on the phone. He would be suspected straight away.

In the end, it was all remarkably simple. He got put through to a news desk and told them his name and that he was a reporter on the *Brookfield Bugle*. He explained roughly what the story was about. They asked for his phone number, saying they might have to ring back with any queries.

"Now hold on," said a voice. "I'll put you through to copy."

"No, no," said Oz, "I don't want it copied. I've got it written here."

"Copy here," said a new voice.

"No, I haven't copied it. Did it all on my own, good typing as well . . ."

"I said copy here. Speak up a bit."

Oz could hear lots of typewriters clattering in the distance.

"Right, I'm ready," said the voice. "Fire away."

Oz then realized he was meant to dictate, so he started, shouting out each word into the telephone, but keeping an eye out, just in case Mr Bott should come in.

Half way through his dictation, the man on the line said he'd had a note from the news desk. They liked his story. Oz had to stand by at the end, and they would ring him back.

Oz felt exhausted when he'd finished dictating, his ear all red and his face flushed. But he had enjoyed it.

There were several words he was sure he had not spelt correctly, such as "geriatric" and "ageism" and he didn't know if "vandals" had one "l" or two. But in dictating, none of that mattered. The clever man at the other end had taken everything down and no doubt had spelt everything correctly.

Oz hardly had to wait a moment before the phone rang. The *Daily Express* was sending a photographer at once, a local freelance, who would be there in half an hour. Oh, and this General Osgood's age. Had he got that? Oz said sorry, that was the only thing he didn't know.

"This is exclusive, isn't it?" said the *Daily Express*. "We pay a lot more for exclusives."

Oz wasn't sure what exclusive meant, but he said, "Yes, of course, very exclusive story."

He took a short pause, to get his breath back and rest his ear, then he rang the *Guardian*. By now, he was experienced in dictating stories.

When he finally finished, he hung up and put the phone back in position. He closed the media resources room, having turned all the lights off, and went back to his grandad's. Very carefully, he put the magic belt back in the wardrobe.

Then he ran home, as fast as his little legs would take him.

"Have you seen the *Guardian* this morning?" said Ossie's mother over breakfast.

"Not had time," said Ossie. "I've got to clear up my breakfast things and get to school, 'cos I want to go and see Grandad . . ."

"There's this weird story, all about the block where Grandad lives. And it's about someone called Mrs Pigg. Don't you know her?"

"Never heard of her," said Ossie.

"I'm sure I've heard Grandad talking about her, that strange woman below him who used to be a suffragette. She seems to have gone absolutely dopey this time. Listen to this Ossie, she's starting an Old Age Pensioners' Liberation Army! It's a scream. According to the story . . ."

"Got to go," said Ossie. "Bye, Mum."

As he went out, he gave her a kiss on the cheek. His mother hardly noticed. She was still reading the *Guardian*, and laughing.

The whole of Grandad's block was in chaos. Two rival television crews were on the lawn, fighting over the best position to film the painted Union Jack, while a group of photographers were pushing each other, trying to get the best shot of the painted walls.

In the centre of all the commotion was Mrs Pigg, giving a press conference.

Ossie eventually pushed his way through the crowds and got to his grandad's front door, but he decided after all not to go in. Better not to disturb him any more.

The *Daily Express* was sticking out of his

grandad's letterbox, so he pulled it out gently and opened it.

The story covered a whole page, most of which was taken up by a huge photograph of Mrs Pigg, standing in the middle of her painted lawn, clenching her fists.

"Power to the Pensioners!" was the main headline.

There was quite a bit Ossie did not recognize, such as quotes from neighbours, and even the Mayor. Then he noticed a reference to "Arthur Osgood, aged 69", who was quoted as saying that he "would not join any Liberation Army, one army had been quite enough for him, and anyway Old Ma Pigg was a barm pot."

That sounded very like Grandad. They must have rung him. And he must have given them his age as sixty-nine.

"What a liar!" thought Ossie. "He's much more than that."

Very carefully, Ossie put the newspaper back in the letterbox.

As Ossie ran out of the gateway of the Sheltered Housing, two taxis screeched to a halt and out got a

Japanese television crew who started running in all directions.

"Heh, doesn't your grandad live in that block?" said Flossie Teacake in class, as they waited for first lesson.

"Could do," said Ossie.

"Look, it's in the *Guardian* today. I brought the page with me."

"These papers just make things up," said Ossie.

"I also saw it on breakfast television. Looked very like his block."

"Could be," said Ossie.

"I've got a great idea," said Flossie. "If you know the block, couldn't *you* do a little story for us? For the *Bugle*, I mean? I'll help you, as I know you can't do joined-up writing very well. And I'll get Dez to write it out neatly in his best handwriting."

"You're not still working on that potty *Bugle*, are you?" said Ossie. "That's kids' stuff. Just playing at being a journalist. I'm saving myself for the real thing."

Ossie took the cutting from Flossie's desk and read it for the first time.

It was quite a short item, compared with the *Daily Express*, but it stuck almost word for word to Oz's own story. But what pleased Ossie most of all was the by-line. "By Oz Good."

The *Guardian* had managed to get his name wrong, but enough of it was right to let the world see that a real, professional, ace reporter had been at work . . .

4

Ossie goes Supersonic!

Every year Ossie and Lucy and their mother went to the Lake District for their summer holidays. They stayed with Grandma Treacle, who was their mother's mother. She lived in a little cottage near Derwentwater, but beside it she had a big barn where Ossie and Lucy slept, if they were good and didn't fight and if it wasn't too cold.

"Ooh, I'm really looking forward to it this year," said Lucy. "Only ten days to go."

"Huh," said Ossie. He was filling in a competition on the back of a soap packet. If you collected twenty coupons and thought of a slogan of no more than fifteen words to sum up why SuperSuds was the most amazing discovery in the history of the universe you got a free journey of a lifetime. Not just one journey of a lifetime. There were three you could choose from. Either Concorde to the West

Indies, the QE2 to New York, or the Orient Express to Venice.

"I hope we can stay in the barn, don't you, Ossie?"

"Huh," he said.

"And she's promised we can go sailing this year. Won't that be fantastic?"

"Great," said Ossie, hardly listening, chewing his pencil and trying to think of a slogan.

"The only thing I don't like," said Lucy, closing the atlas in which she had been studying a map of the Lake District, "is having to go by train."

"I think I'll go by Concorde," said Ossie.

"To the Lake District?" said Lucy. "Don't be silly."

"I don't care where it goes. I just want to go on Concorde."

"You can't go to the railway station and say three tickets on Concorde to Keswick, please," said Lucy. "Sometimes, Ossie Osgood, I think you're potty."

"I've been on a train lots of times," said Ossie, studying the coloured photographs on the back of the soap packet. "This Orient thing looks a very old-fashioned train. Who wants to go on that? And look at all those soppy clothes they're wearing. I'll make the Orient Express my number three. Don't want to win that."

"You won't win anything," said Lucy. "You've never won anything in your whole life."

"This QE2 boat looks pretty good, Lucy. Whatjathink? Only trouble is, I have been on a boat, many a time."

"What a liar," said Lucy. "You've never been on a boat."

"On Derwentwater, ha ha ha," said Ossie.

"Those are just titchy little boats, going round and round," said Lucy. "I'd love to go on the QE2. It's like being in a luxury hotel. Put that as your number one, Ossie. Go on. Then I'll come with you."

"No chance. Concorde is what I want to travel on more than anything else in this whole world. I'll choose that. Hope it doesn't clash with going to the Lake District."

"You haven't even got the slogan yet," said Lucy. "Or the twenty coupons."

"That's easy."

"It is for you. Being so filthy. Mum has to buy soap powder all the time."

"Right, that's it," said Ossie. "When I go on Concorde, *you* are not coming with me."

In the playground next day, everyone was talking about their summer holiday plans. And in some cases, showing off about their holiday plans.

"Yes, we're driving across France," said Flossie Teacake.

"You've told me," said Ossie.

"Yes, all the way across France. I'm so excited."

"Get a new tune, will you. You're boring."

"We're going to this beautiful cottage. It's near Lyons," said Flossie.

"I hope they bite you," said Ossie.

"What are you talking about? You're just jealous."

"We're going to the Lake District. My gran has this fantastic barn, really great, and we're allowed to sleep in it . . ."

"Big deal," said Flossie. "We sleep in the back of our estate car, while it's travelling. We just go zoom zoom across France . . ."

"Huh, who wants to travel in a car? I'm probably going to travel on Concorde this year, not definite, but it's pretty definite, probably."

"You ever been to France?" asked Flossie, ignoring Ossie's reference to Concorde.

"Sort of," said Ossie. "Driven near it."

"What a fibber. I know you haven't ever driven to France. You know how I know, Ossie Osgood?"

"Come on, tell me, clever clogs."

"Because you haven't even got a car!"

Flossie walked off, triumphant. She knew she'd got him this time.

Ossie had no reply. His mother not only did not have a car, she had never even passed her driving test.

Ossie had sworn his mother to secrecy, making her keep the garage door permanently closed, so no one could see the emptiness inside, hoping that no one in his class would ever find out.

"Now Flossie will tell everybody, rotten lot."

On the way home, Desmond also brought up the subject of summer holidays, as if by chance.

"Yeh, usual place," said Desmond. "They do us very well there. We know all the waiters and the best places to eat and how to get seats round the pool before anyone else and everyfink."

"Not Benidorm *again*," said Ossie. "Doesn't it get pretty boring, year after year?"

"Not as boring as the stupid old Lake District, year after year. Bleeding perishing. Can't sunbathe there, can you. Or swim in the sea. Or stay up late in the hotel and drink wine. I'm allowed to, you know, when *we're* on holiday."

"You got the runs last year," said Ossie.

"No, I didn't."

"Yes, you did. You came home and had five days off with the runs. Your mum told my mum."

"Well, only a little bit. I was just putting it on, to get off school."

"Putting it out, you mean. I told everyone in the class you had the runs."

"Well, when you go abroad, you have to expect little things like that, in a strange country, eating their funny food. Not that *you* would know anything about that, Ossie."

"Whatchamean?"

"You have never been abroad in your whole life."

"Yes, I have."

"Where?"

"Scotland."

"That's not abroad. I mean a foreign country. I *know* you haven't, so don't lie. Your mum told my mum. So there. Got you. Well sussed."

On Saturday morning, Ossie as usual was doing his grandfather's weekend shopping. This time he was getting it done as quickly as possible. He had been invited to spend the day with Desmond.

They were now good friends again, especially after Desmond let slip that his dad had just got a video camera, one you could take real films with, then play them back instantly on the television screen.

In the queue at the supermarket, as Ossie was waiting to check out, he seemed to hear even more people talking about their summer holidays. And all of them were going somewhere by plane.

There was one thing which neither Flossie nor Desmond had ever found out, one terrible admission which so far Ossie had managed to keep secret from the world.

"I bet I'm the only twelve-year-old boy in the whole of this country who has never been on an aeroplane."

Ossie trudged along the street to his grandad's, carrying the shopping, imagining himself getting on a plane, being strapped in. He put the shopping down and his arms out, just to get the motion right.

Best of all, so Desmond and all his friends always said, you got a meal on the plane. Actually on a plane. A little tray, all to yourself.

"Amazing how they can do that. On a plane. A hot meal. Wish I'd been on a plane."

He picked up the bags and carried on.

"Desmond says he once had chips on a plane. And a hamburger. Bet he was making it up. Bet he just said it, to make me jealous.

"And he also says you get free Coke. What a liar, that Desmond. No one ever gives you free Coke.

"But how would I know? I haven't been on a plane. I haven't been abroad. I haven't done anything exciting in this whole world."

"Grandad, what's France like?"

Ossie was putting the shopping away.

"Smelly," said Grandad.

That was one thing about discussing foreign parts with Grandad. He always told the truth, not like some people Ossie could mention.

"They stink of garlic and they smoke those nasty cigarettes."

"Flossie Teacake says it's terrific. She goes every year with her family."

"Mind you," said his grandad, putting a boiled sweet in his mouth, "it was in 1943 that I was last in

France. I was in a train and it was the middle of the night. All the same, I didn't like the look, the sight nor the smell of that France."

"What's Spain like?"

"Full of Spaniards. Haven't you seen it on television?"

"No, but have you been, personally, you know, yourself?"

"North Africa, I been there."

"Heh, tell me about that, Grandad, tell me everything you can remember."

Ossie always found it a great consolation to be able to say that someone in his family had been somewhere foreign and exotic and exciting.

For years, he'd boasted about his grandfather's best exploit of all. In the war, Grandad had been in a submarine. He had a medal, somewhere, locked up, to prove it. None of Ossie's friends knew anyone who had been anywhere near a real submarine. It had kept him going throughout the whole of his primary school years.

"Think hard, Grandad. What was North Africa *really* like?"

"Full of sand," said Grandad.

Ossie's face rather fell. Not much to boast about, having seen a lot of sand. Every year Desmond came back from Benidorm, boasting about the brill sand.

Ossie decided to ring up and cancel Desmond's. He would only have to put up with a lot more boasting about holidays in Spain and swimming pools and how many planes Desmond had flown in over the years and all the marvellous aeroplane meals he had guzzled. Probably even show them on their new video.

"I haven't even *seen* a plane, never mind been on one," said Ossie, walking back to his own home. "Not close up anyway. I wouldn't recognize one if I met one in my porridge."

That was one of his grandmother Treacle's sayings.

"Now where's that place where you can look at planes? Flossie got taken there once with her dad. But I wouldn't be allowed to go there, not on my own. Too young. Too little. That's what they always say. Snot fair."

Ossie stopped at the end of his street. His mother and Lucy did not expect him home. Why couldn't he go and look at planes for the day? All on his own.

Ossie turned round and hurried back to his grandfather's.

As he was creeping into the wardrobe, something fell down with a clank and a clink. He picked it up and found it was a medallion, with a submarine on it. So it had been true.

He put it back and listened. His grandad was busy watching *Saturday Superstore* on television.

"I want to be eighteen, this very moment, oh please," said Ossie, closing his eyes. "Big enough and old enough to go to London on my own . . ."

Oz got off the tube at Heathrow. It had been quite an easy journey, surprisingly easy, both the train and the tube, but then when you're eighteen and a young man of the world, travelling is not difficult.

He was looking for the way to the Observation Roof, which was the place Flossie had told him to go to, a special area where you can stand and watch all the aeroplanes, landing and taking off.

"Oh, no, forgotten my camera. Wish I'd brought it with me. Nobody will ever believe I've been here."

First of all, he had a look round all the shops and gift places, the banks and the nurseries, the cafeterias and bookshops.

"It's like a huge town. I never knew it was so big. And all these foreign people, speaking foreign languages. You don't actually need to go abroad. Abroad has come here."

Then he queued up for a cup of coffee, but stopped when he saw the prices. He'd only found enough money, in his eighteen-year-old trousers, for his return fares.

"It's so hot. I feel I'm getting a tan."

He followed a sign saying "Passport Control", thinking that might be where passports were handed out, but he was stopped by two fierce security guards. They asked Oz for his aeroplane ticket and his passport.

One of them started talking into a pocket radio, looking at Oz, giving out what sounded like a description, so Oz quickly turned round and disappeared into the crowds.

"Don't want to end up in prison," he thought. "Not when I've got to be home with Mum and Lucy in time for tea."

★

Oz found he had wandered behind a roped-off area, where two girls and a boy about his age, not much more than eighteen or nineteen, were standing chatting to each other.

"Hi," said Oz, being friendly. "Where you off to?"

"Oh, just a spin," said the boy. "My grandmother's outing. Not sure where we're going yet."

As they stood chatting, an official came out of a doorway, all smiles and charm, practically bowing to the floor, and gave out three tickets, one to each of the three teenagers.

"Oh sorry, I didn't know there were four of you," he said, apologetically. "I'll get another ticket. Terribly sorry, m'Lord."

He then bustled through another doorway.

"He must think I'm a pop singer," said Oz. "There is one called Lord Sutch, isn't there? And I've heard of someone called Duke something or other. And isn't there a singer called Prince? Actually, I'm always being mistaken for someone famous. I have been confused with Steve Davis. But yous lot can call me Oz."

Oz extended his hand and shook hands with each

of them in turn and carried on chatting. When you're eighteen, you have the confidence and experience and style to do such things, so Oz thought. "Can I come with you? As long as we're home for tea, I don't think my mum will mind."

"I don't see why not," said the boy, smiling. "I was told I could bring a few friends. As my sister's got one, you can come as well."

"Thanks," said Oz. "That's well smart of you."

All three teenagers pricked up their ears, interested to hear some new slang.

"Actually, I've never been on a plane before," said Oz. "Amazing isn't it, getting to twelve, sorry I mean eighteen, and never flying. I've been on the dodgems, the waltzer, lots of merry-go-rounds, the big wheel, the ghost train, round Derwentwater on the launch, that's really good, but I've never flown. Do you have to wear a parachute?"

The official came back with the extra ticket and gave it to Oz, bowing once again, almost scraping the floor. Oz noticed that in fact a piece of red carpet had been put down.

"You'd think we were Royalty," said Oz.

All three of them burst out laughing, much to

Oz's pleasure. He did like to give value for money, as his mother always encouraged. It was a way of thanking people, especially if they were being kind enough to take him somewhere.

Two security men, walking past, suddenly stopped and looked at Oz, recognizing his description. One of them started talking quickly into his radio.

"Oh, no," said Oz. "I haven't got a passport. I've been stopped already. I'd better go. Sorry about that. It's such a shame, I've never been on a plane before . . ."

The young man looked at Oz, and his two companions, and then he smiled.

"We're only going to Scotland. No need for passports."

He walked over to the security guards, very confidently.

"I say, this gentleman is in our party. He's with us. Is that clear?"

"Oh, sorry, sir. Of course, sir. No problem, m'Lord. Your Ladyship. Have a good flight."

As they spoke, another official appeared, this time in what looked like fancy dress uniform, with lots of gold braid, and he escorted all four teenagers through a side door and into a little hallway.

"This way, please, your Highnesses."

"Amazing, isn't it," said Oz. "My record must be zooming up the charts. It was Lord a few moments ago. Now it's your Highness. I must watch *Top of the Pops* this week. See if I'm number one."

"I say, you have to place your hand luggage here, I'm afraid," said the official. "Only a formality, har har har, but has to be done. Has to be seen to be done. Can't break rules, can we? What what."

They had come to a conveyor belt and a rectangular metal doorway. Five uniformed attendants were lined up beside it, as if to attention, as if they'd been waiting for Oz's party to arrive.

The young man put a camera on the conveyor belt and the two girls their handbags.

"Your belt, sir," said one of the attendants, looking very officiously at Oz.

Oz stopped. He couldn't take his belt off. That would be the end of everything, even if he just unbuckled it for a moment.

"Er, I'm sorry, I can't . . ."

Everyone stared at Oz, wondering why he

suddenly looked so worried. They could see that his belt was a particularly fine one, very heavy and ornate. It was so big that it might well contain any number of secret compartments and devices, and probably would make a very handy weapon.

"Jolly fine belt you've got there," said one of the girls, rather nervously.

"It's my grandad's actually," said Oz. "Great sentimental value. Been in the family for yonkers. I was told never to let anyone else touch it."

"Yes, we have things like that in our family," said the young man.

Everyone was still staring at Oz, especially the security people.

"Me mum said I'd never to take it off," said Oz, almost like a little boy.

"Look, be a good chap, do let him pass through," said the young man. "It is just a family flight, a private trip. I can vouch for it that my friend Oz is not carrying anything offensive."

"Only my language is offensive," said Oz. "My gran tells me off all the time. She says I've never to use the phrase 'Oh God' ever again."

The young man put his arm round Oz's shoulder.

"Yes, my grandmother is very much the same."

All the attendants stood back very respectfully while Oz and his party were waved through.

Oz could hardly believe his eyes. The plane waiting for them was so familiar to him, its line so well known, its shape instantly recognizable. Oz felt he was meeting a friend, someone he had known all his life.

"Concorde!" Oz almost shouted out the word.

"Yes, good idea, isn't it?" said the boy. "My grandmother has never been on it. It's been organized as a special treat for her eighty-fifth birthday."

As they were admiring Concorde, a large black limousine rolled silently across the tarmac from another direction, a little flag flying from its bonnet. Even before it stopped, a man jumped out and was standing to attention, his hand on the rear door, the second the car halted.

Oz hardly looked at the dignified old lady who got out of the car, though there seemed to be something familiar about her face. He was too busy admiring Concorde.

She was escorted towards the plane and was allowed to be first on. Oz really wanted to be first, but he decided to let her get ahead. It might be a bit rude to push her out of the way, as she was eighty-five, and it was her birthday, and he was just a guest.

"In our house," Oz told his new friends as they all followed on to the plane, "you can do anything on your birthday. Cry, and no one tells you off. No need to do the dishes. All meals made for you. It's really lush. No washing up either. Do you get birthday bumps in your house?"

"Don't think we do that, actually," said the boy's sister.

"It is a bit noisy, especially if you live in a small house. Do you live in a flat, or a house?"

"Sort of," said the girl.

"I like your grandma's purple hat," said Oz. "And her purple coat. My gran wears stuff like that. Really old-fashioned. Did she get it from a jumble? My gran gets all her things from jumbles."

"I don't think my grandmother frequents jumble sales," said the boy.

"Funny grandmother," said Oz.

"Oh yes she does," said his sister. "She often goes to one near the Castle of Mey. What about those embroidered cushions she bought at the jumble sale at Caithness?"

"Oh, that's true," said the boy, "I forgot."

"So she is an ordinary gran after all," said Oz.

"Perfectly ordinary," said the boy.

"Except she does have her own castle," said one of the other girls, and they all smiled.

"Sheltered Housing is amazing these days," said Oz.

Oz was slightly disappointed to find that Concorde's seats were quite small, not that he had very much to compare them with, but he had expected a bit more leg room. However, as there were so few passengers, there was ample space for everyone to walk round the plane and inspect all the fittings, which is what he had been doing.

"Is that a digital clock?" said Oz, pointing to a little screen. "Why does it say 'Mach 2'? Must be stuck. These cheap digitals are always going wrong."

"That means we've passed the speed of sound,"

said a stewardess.

Oz could hardly believe it, as it all seemed so silent and comfortable. He had felt the plane take off, very quickly, with a roar like a racing car, but since then he had been busy fiddling with a sort of Walkman set which he had found fixed to his seat. It seemed to have about five stations he could tune in to.

He'd also been looking at all the free things they'd been given: Concorde socks, Concorde photographs, Concorde luggage labels in grey leather, Concorde writing paper, Concorde envelopes and a Concorde Certificate to prove he had flown supersonic.

"We're now over the Atlantic," said the stewardess. "Flying at sixty thousand feet, and a speed of one thousand, three hundred and fifty miles an hour, but we'll drop speed soon as we sweep round the North of Scotland."

"God, it's quicker than the tube," said Oz. "I mean, oh goodness, it's quicker than the tube. Sorry about that. Hope your granny didn't hear."

"No, she's busy having a drink," said one of the girls.

"We're hoping, if visibility is OK, to be able to see Balmoral Castle as we fly over," said the stewardess. "It's a special surprise for the Queen Mother."

"Well, it will be," said Oz. "To see me flying over her head."

Champagne was served in crystal goblets. Oz was surprised. He'd been waiting for instant coffee in plastic cups, which is what Desmond always boasted about.

All the teenagers had some, so Oz thought he had better try a glass as well. He had never tasted champagne before, but he didn't want to mention it, just in case his new friends thought he might be the sort of person who had never been anywhere exciting in his life.

"Not bad, this," said Oz. "Bit like Coke, without the colouring."

No sooner had he finished his glass, than they came round again. So Oz took some more, just to be sociable.

"Do you realize we're twice the height of Everest," said one of the girls, drinking her champagne very slowly.

"I didn't know Everest could fly," said Oz, drinking rather quickly.

He tried to look out of the window, but could only see a few clouds. The windows anyway were very small.

"Do you think we'll be there before we've started," said Oz, "and meet ourselves coming back?"

"You're thinking about the speed of light," said the boy. "We're just going supersonic."

Oz was feeling a bit confused, possibly even a bit dizzy.

"If I shout," said Oz, "then run down the aisle, will I get there before my voice gets there?"

"Very possibly," said one of the girls. "Especially if you have any more champagne . . ."

Oz must have dozed off slightly, because he awoke to find one of the cabin crew laying out a stiff, white tablecloth in front of him.

"No thanks," said Oz. "I don't want a haircut."

The steward then brought very heavy silver cutlery, Wedgwood bone china cup and saucer and

Royal Doulton plates.

"Oh, it's a banquet, is it?" said Oz. "Desmond never mentioned no banquet."

The first course appeared to be little squares of bread, about the size of postage stamps, with different sorts of fillings on top.

"Do you eat these," said Oz, "or stick them in your album?" Everyone laughed, which pleased Oz.

"Don't you like canapés?" said one of the girls.

"Never had them actually," said Oz. "I think my grandad used to have one, to cover up his motor-bike."

Oz took a bite and then made a face.

"Ugh, this fish hasn't been cooked," he said.

"It's smoked salmon, that's why," said one of the girls.

"Nobody smokes in our house," said Oz. "That's why I've never had them. I get asthma you see, at least I did when I was little, about twelve, so we never allow any sort of smoking in our house . . ."

The next course was again fish and this time, so Oz thought, the fish was not just uncooked, but still alive. He picked up a lobster claw and looked at it very carefully.

"It won't bite me, will it?" said Oz. "And what's all these little black ballbearings for?"

He declined to try it, just in case he got hurt, but he studied the menu to see what was next. It said "Tournedos".

"Sounds more like a weather forecast than a menu," said Oz.

It turned out to be fillet steak, which Oz loved, as he liked any sort of steak, if it was well done.

He did think about asking for HP sauce to go on top, or even tomato ketchup, but looking around at all the smart people and crew, the posh tableware and seats, he decided perhaps they wouldn't have bottles of sauce on Concorde.

"Are you all enjoying your flight, hmm?" said the young man's grandmother.

She was walking down the aisle, looking from side to side. She seemed to be waving to people as she did so, at least lifting her hand in a gracious gesture each time she stopped and spoke to someone.

"Does she do this all the time?" said Oz to his friends.

"Never stops," said a girl. "It's her job."

"No, I mean, does she go on Concorde trips all the time?"

"It's her first flight."

"Same here," said Oz. "Think I'll try and get my mum to book me a trip when I'm eighteen, I mean eighty-five. You're all invited."

"Thanks," said one of the girls. "That's really cool."

"And how are *you* getting on, hmm?"

The gracious grandmother was now bending over Oz. He could smell her perfume. Admire her pearls close up. And she did have a very nice smile.

"Trific, thanks for inviting me. Sorry I didn't send you a card. Didn't know it was your birthday."

"Oh, not to worry," she said.

"Did you get very many?"

"I should think about a hundred thousand."

"Lucky beggar," said Oz. "I only got five, and I know two of them were from my mum, just to make them look more."

There wasn't much room in the cockpit of Concorde, but the view was incredible.

Oz had asked if he could sit down behind the pilot, and the grandmother said she was sure he could. Everyone else wanted to do the same.

"We're now over Cumbria," said the pilot. "Look, in the distance, you should soon be able to see Windermere."

"Don't be stupid," said Oz. "Are you wandering?"

"Sorry?" said the pilot, pulling a few switches, setting a few knobs, reading a few instruments.

"That's never Windermere," repeated Oz. "You need your eyesight tested."

The teenagers were all looking at Oz, thinking this time he was being a little bit rude, especially for a last-minute guest, whom they didn't really know.

"Windermere is long and thin," said Oz. "Don't you know that? Hold on, just a few seconds, till we get nearer. Yup. I thought so. It's Derwentwater. You can always tell Derwentwater because it's sort of squat and square, whereas all the other Lakes are long and thin.

"Look, now you can see the islands on Derwentwater. And there's Keswick."

The pilot consulted a map, which was rotating in

front of him, and then he looked up again.

"You're perfectly right," said the pilot.

"And we should now be passing over Skiddaw," said Oz. "I've been up there many a time."

"Right again," said the pilot, consulting his map.

"If you want any more tips, any information, any gen on the Lake District," said Oz, "just give me a ring. I'm in the book."

Before they left the plane, one of the stewardesses came round all the teenagers and asked them if they'd like her to post their Concorde envelopes.

"Now, should I send one to Desmond? No, he doesn't deserve it. Or Flossie? She wouldn't know what Concorde was. She only ever goes on holidays by car, poor thing."

On his special Concorde writing paper, Oz wrote out his own Concorde message.

"Having a good time. Wish you were here. Love, Oz."

He enclosed with it his Concorde Supersonic Flight Certificate.

Then he addressed it. To Oswald Osgood, Esq.

★

Ossie was home well in time for tea. The journey back had been even quicker than the journey there.

His grandfather was out, so there was no need to sneak in this time, but Ossie made sure, as always, that he hung the belt up in its special place and closed the wardrobe, very carefully.

He wanted no one to know the wardrobe had been entered, just in case he ever needed to use the magic belt again, one of these days.

"Have you seen the newspaper?" said his mother next morning.

"Too much to do to read the paper," said Ossie.

"For the Queen Mother's eighty-fifth birthday treat, they organized a special trip on Concorde. Wasn't that a good idea?"

"Trific," said Ossie.

"And she took some of her grandchildren, Lord Linley and Lady Sarah Armstrong-Jones and some of their young friends. What a lovely thing to do. Look, here's a photograph of them."

"Sounds well smart," said Ossie. "But I'd rather go with you on the train to the Lake District any time. Much more exciting."

"Creep," said Lucy.

"All you do on Concorde is guzzle," said Ossie.
"So I'm told . . ."